Love Walks In

ALOHA ROMANCE SERIES • BOOK SEVEN

CHRIS KENISTON

Indie House Publishing

MORE BOOKS
By Chris Keniston

Hart Land
Heather
Lily
Violet
Iris
Hyacinth
Rose
Calytrix
Zinnia
Poppy
Picture Perfect

Farraday Country
Adam
Brooks
Connor
Declan
Ethan
Finn
Grace
Hannah
Ian
Jamison
Keeping Eileen
Loving Chloe
Morgan
Neil

Honeymoon Series
Honeymoon for One
Honeymoon for Three
Honeymoon for Four
Honeymoon for Five

Aloha Romance Series:
Aloha Texas
Almost Paradise
Mai Tai Marriage
Dive Into You
Look of Love
Love by Design
Love Walks In
Shell Game
Flirting with Paradise

Surf's Up Flirts:
(Aloha Series Companions)
Shall We Dance
Love on Tap
Head Over Heels
Perfect Match
Just One Kiss
It Had to Be You
Cat's Meow

ACKNOWLEDGEMENTS

Originally written for an autism fundraising project, *Love Walks In* is very dear to my heart.

This book would never have come to pass without the help of Nancy Green, a wonderful woman who shared story after story and read page after page to help me get this story right. Thank you to Brian McNeill, a real life Adam and an example to young and old on the true meaning of friendship and human kindness.

Local unified basketball teams such as the one in this book do exist and are highly successful. Which brings me to one last thank you and congratulations—to Kevin Green. At the time of the writing of this book Kevin and his teammates had returned from the 2015 Los Angeles Special Olympics World Games with a Gold Medal in Unified Sports Experience Basketball! Way to go!

I hope you enjoy *Love Walks In* and thanks for reading!

CHAPTER ONE

"Tom, you would have loved living in this house." Seated at the café table nestled in the corner of her living room, Annette Deluca held the silver frame encasing her family's photo. She remembered the day in 3-D Technicolor. Adam's fifth birthday. Corralling her offspring for a photograph had taken more effort than organizing the entire party at the popular children's venue. What the picture didn't reveal was the near headlock it had taken for her to pin down their son for two minutes nor the gentle pressure with which her husband Tom's hands held their daughter in place. Yet somehow Tom's assistant had managed to coax a smile out of the two siblings, creating the perfect family picture. Oh, how Annette missed that.

With the windows wide open, the wind carried the sound of the distant waves crashing ashore and dropped them beside her, opening another floodgate of memories. Summers by the beach. Winters diving in Hawaii or the Barrier Reef. Christmas in the mountains. They'd done it all before the children were born and then done it again as a family. "Do you have any idea how much I miss you?" she asked the man in the photo.

A gull swooping past the window caught her attention. Focusing on the broad wingspan as the bird glided away from the house and out to sea, she gave herself a mental shake. The last thing her late husband would want her to do is spend her days living in the past. "Time to get back to ringing in the season." This year she thought she'd follow the lead of advertisers on television and get the house all cheery with Christmas spirit now, instead of waiting for after Thanksgiving. Over the weekend, she and the kids would bring out the tree and spend some family time hanging the ornaments and tinsel, and maybe even stringing some popcorn—the way they did when Adam and Bethany were really young. Pushing herself upright, Annette set the frame on the shelf where it belonged. Surrounded by the wealth of family photos that helped keep the memories strong, she shoved aside the melancholy and opened another box of holiday decorations.

The first Christmas without Tom had been difficult. Thank heaven for Maggie. Annette's household manager had become indispensable. Caring for the children day and night, taking on the role of mother, while Annette pushed her way through physical therapy and recovery. It was so hard to believe she'd survived that horrible crash. But she had with Maggie's help. And then there was the entire Everrett clan. All of them, and what seemed like half the navy's Special Forces, looked out for her and her children in those dark days after the plane crash that took Tom's life and left her fighting for hers.

And Lord bless Maile Everrett. Opening her home for the holidays had made the void caused by Tom's absence a little easier to bear. Annette and her kids had still felt the hurt, but most of their smiles had been genuine, and that was due to the warmhearted matriarch. And, of course, the Everrett family's ever-faithful German shepherd, Gunny, who had done as much for bringing back the spark to her son's life as Maile's grown son had.

"Wow, the water is perfect today." Maggie wrapped a beach towel around her, tucking in the corner as she crossed the threshold.

"This is Hawaii." Annette laughed. "The water is perfect every day."

"I know. But, after so many years living in L.A., I keep expecting the ocean to feel like an ice pond in Antarctica."

"Not going to happen." Prominently placing the antique Santa's sleigh and reindeer she'd retrieved from the box on the minimalist mantel, Annette shook her head at her friend.

The familiar sound of her cell carrier's ring tone played. She really needed to pick a better tune. Her phone always sounded like a television commercial for her provider. Glancing quickly at the screen, her heart gave a small stutter as the name of her son's school popped up. "Hello?"

"Mrs. Deluca, this is Harriett from the principal's office."

Her mind ran full speed ahead. All the horrible possibilities for a phone call from school tripped and shoved their way over the benign and more likely reasons. "Yes?"

"We've had a little … incident."

Okay. *Incident* is way better than *accident*, and Harriett's tone, while stern with a hint of frustration, gave no indication that Annette needed to be racing to the emergency room. "How little?"

"Adam has been in a fight."

"A what?" Her son didn't fight. The kid was a card-carrying member of Future Pacifists of America. Hug the trees and save the whales too. "Are you sure?"

"Excuse me?"

"Never mind. What happened?"

"I think we should discuss this in person."

"Very well. I'll be there in a few minutes."

"Mrs. Deluca?"

"Yes?"

"Bring a clean shirt."

Clean shirt?

"And pants. Your son's have seen better days."

Another number changed on the digital clock. Brian would be home in a few minutes. Sometimes Michael Becker wondered who attending a new school was more stressful on, him or his son. So far it was a toss-up. He'd hoped mainstreaming middle school in Hawaii would be easier on Brian than in the large Dade County public school system. All his son wanted was to be like other kids his age. To go to a regular school, have friends, be invited to parties. There was even talk of a girlfriend.

Mike scrubbed his hand down his face. Hawaii might be Paradise, but he wasn't holding out for miracles. Or maybe he was. Normal people didn't turn their entire world upside down if they weren't hoping for something.

Awake since four o'clock this morning for a conference call with L.A., Mike seriously doubted the wisdom of his choice to live in the Hawaii-Aleutian time zone. Working for a Fortune 500 company on a global IT project had its perks and problems. He could telecommute from the house and be home for Brian. On the downside Mike could be attached to his computer at all hours of the day and night seven days a week. Or the blasted phone. And if Singapore didn't have the numbers run for him in the next minute, they would just bloody well have to wait for him to do his part. No way could he ignore Brian's arrival after school. For the last twelve years, routine had been critical in every aspect of his life. Even as a baby Brian didn't adapt to variations in the daily schedule. Karen had made it all look so easy. From sunrise to bedtime, everything ran like clockwork.

Now, as soon as Brian walked through the door, the well-planned and practiced system kicked into gear. To the minute. No room for the slightest deviation. Snack. Homework. TV. *Homework.* Mike pinched the bridge of his nose.

The last digit flipped on the clock as Mike and Brian's neighbor pulled in the driveway. "Bless her."

Not many people understood Brian's need for order and routine and schedules. Heaven forbid his ride home from school decided to stop at the grocery store for a gallon of milk or try a shortcut to save time. The slightest detour always spelled disaster. But his neighbor Liz got it. She picked up Brian at the exact same spot at the exact same time and drove home the exact same route, and, so far, Liz was the only thing about the new school and the new routine that was going well.

His work cell resting on the desk buzzed. Glancing down, Mike saw the long string of numbers—Singapore. *Not good.* Preferring to use chat or email, it wasn't normal for the offshore team to call. This could only mean trouble. Reluctantly he grabbed the phone. "Becker."

"Good afternoon, Mike," the caller began. Always frustrated by the formality of the greeting and the acknowledgment of the time difference, he replied with the standard, "And good morning to you." After all, Singapore was eighteen hours ahead—already the next day. What he really wanted though was to hurry up this conversation—get to the point. The last thing he needed was a lengthy conversation with Brian about to walk in the door.

The sound of a car door slamming broke into his thoughts, followed by another, and Mike's head snapped up. Liz normally watched Brian walk to the door and waited for Mike to wave back. The routine didn't call for her to get out of the car and walk with Brian. *Not good.* With a quick "I need to go. Send me an email," he cut short the call and dropped the phone.

Tempted to hurry outside to find out what happened, instead Mike bit his cheeks and waited for Brian to open the door as usual. The second Brian appeared in the doorway, Mike knew the slight change had been enough to throw his son off his game. Brian's gaze remained on the floor, watching his feet as he moved farther into the house.

"Time for your snack. Would you like ice cream, an apple, or chips?" Mike hoped falling into the familiar repartee would be enough to get his son back on track.

Quietly Brian continued to the kitchen, his gaze still cast downward.

Before continuing with the cycle of asking three times, Mike leaned toward Liz and whispered, "Wait for me in the living room."

Liz nodded and, passing behind him, made her way to the other room. Much to Mike's relief, the remainder of the snack-time routine fell into place. Once he'd placed the apple slices on the table, Brian seemed to have recovered from the small shift.

Wiping his hands down the side of his slacks, Mike took a seat in the living room, drew in a fortifying breath, and hoped whatever Liz had to say wasn't going to turn their world upside down again. "What happened?"

"There was a fight at school."

"Fight?" Mike sprang to his feet and turned to bolt back into the kitchen, not sure how he could have missed signs of a physical encounter.

Liz grabbed his wrist. "Not Brian."

What did she mean? What was the point of disrupting everything to tell him someone else had a fight at school? "I don't understand."

"It looks like your son has a new champion."

CHAPTER TWO

The sky-blue halls of the Kona Middle School normally gave Annette a sense of calm, but this afternoon they did little to ease the anxiety building with every step. Just the other day she'd read an article on delayed delinquent behavior in young teens after the death of a parent. Was this about that?

The short walk to the principal's office seemed interminable. The moment Annette turned the corner, her eyes fell on her son. Slumped in the last of a line of chairs along the office wall, Adam sat with his head tilted back, holding an ice pack to his face. The collar on his polo shirt hung awkwardly, and she could see dark smudges all over him from across the room. Not until she was directly in front of her son did she see the torn pants and the equally disheveled boy on the other side of him. "What happened?"

"It was his fault." Adam pointed a thumb at the other kid.

"Was not," an angry voice mumbled through a split lip.

As much as she hated to admit relief, Annette was fairly confident the dark smudges on her son's shirt could be attributed to the other kid's bloody lip. "I didn't ask whose fault it was. What happened?"

"Oh, good, you're here." Harriett came out from behind the front counter. "The principal is in his office. Do you want to take a minute for Adam to change his clothes?"

Annette had brought a shirt and pants, as requested, but she much preferred finding out what had happened than she was concerned about Adam's appearance. "No, let's face the music."

Harriett stepped to one side and waved Annette and

Adam across the bullpen of office desks to the closed door of childhood dread. "Go right in. He's expecting you."

Annette rapped lightly on the door and then turned the knob.

"Come in." Ted Sparks was a jovial man with an easygoing grin. But not today. "Please take a seat."

Nerves still on edge, Annette eased into one of the chairs in front of the massive oak desk. Adam slumped into the seat beside her.

"We don't tolerate fighting." Fingers steepled in front of him, the principal shifted his gaze from Adam to her. "Normally turning to fisticuffs is an automatic suspension."

"Normally?" she asked cautiously.

"First offense is up to the principal's discretion." The man eyed Adam. "Do you have something to say in your defense?"

"No, sir."

"I see here"—the principal held up a single piece of paper—"that you're not in any classes with Eddie."

Eddie. Annette quickly ran through overheard conversations but didn't recognize the name.

"No, sir."

The stern-looking man glanced at Annette over the sheet of paper in his hand before turning back to Adam. "Does this have anything to do with Brian Becker?"

Adam's eyes widened just long enough for both Annette and the principal to realize he'd hit the nail on the head. But who was Brian Becker?

Adam straightened in his seat. "Brian wasn't part of the fight."

"I see." The usually cordial twinkle in Principal Ted's eyes gleamed once again, as he leaned back in his chair. "I think we can let this go with a warning. And perhaps an essay on problem resolution without the use of violence."

Adam's mouth drew into a thin line, but he nodded anyhow. "Thank you, sir."

On the way outside, Annette noticed the other boy, Eddie, had company. A big guy in jeans, a sweat-soaked work shirt, and what looked to be steel-tipped shoes sat scowling beside the kid. She had to wonder who would dole out the harsher punishment, the good-natured principal or the father who looked to be royally ticked off at missing work. She almost felt sorry for the kid.

Seat belt snapped, turning out of the parking lot, Annette uttered the first words spoken since leaving the principal's office. "Why did you give Eddie a split lip?"

Adam's mouth curled in a triumphant smile. "I did, didn't I?"

Men. "Answer the question."

Adam shifted in his seat, ran his hand along his jaw, and looked to the roof of the car as though expecting the answer to appear etched on the ceiling.

"Does it hurt?" She would put more ice on his chin once they got home.

"Nah." He dropped his hand to his side. "Eddie hits like a girl."

A startled chuckle erupted, and Annette didn't even try to hold it back. For a second she thought she could hear her husband laughing beside her. "Spill. What happened?"

"We've got a new kid in school."

She nodded, waiting for more.

"His name is Brian. He's smart in a weird sort of way."

"Weird?"

"Yeah. He remembers everything. I mean *everything*. In history class the teacher read a passage from one of the pages, then asked a question. Before anyone could raise their hand, Brian answered."

"Just called out the answer?"

Adam shook his head. "Mom, he recited back the entire page. It's almost scary. I don't have math with him, but I heard, when the class has to do calculations, he does them in his head. Fast. Really fast."

A myriad of possibilities played in her thoughts. The old cliché, a fine line between genius and insanity. Though her maternal gut told her this was more complicated than a weird smart kid. "So why did you have a fight with this Eddie character?"

"He's an obnoxious ass—"

"Adam."

"Well, he is. He thinks his shit doesn't stink."

The desire to get to the bottom of the situation won out over the urge to reprove her son's inappropriately colorful vocabulary. She bit her tongue and waited.

"Him and all his friends are always picking on kids. They rule the lunchroom. The minute one of the volunteers isn't looking, Eddie's knocking over someone's tray or tripping a kid walking by."

"Picks on those he's intimidated by."

"No." Adam shook his head vehemently. "He picks mostly on the geeks."

"The *smart* geeks. I'm guessing he's not the best student."

Adam shrugged. "I don't know. Maybe. But he and his friends keep taunting this kid."

"How?"

"Stupid stuff. Someone said the other day how Eddie told Brian to go kiss the elevator. And he did. And that he seemed happy, like he thought it would make him Eddie's friend."

"You didn't see this?"

Brian shook his head. "And yesterday it was cleaning spit, but today I was in the hall, when I heard Eddie and his friends tell Brian to kiss Katie Russo."

Uh-oh. "Did he?"

Adam nodded. "They told him that she really liked him. Wanted to be his girlfriend. She was nearby, and Eddie called her over. Everyone was hurrying to get to class before the bell rang, and I couldn't get across the hall fast enough to stop him."

The way her son glanced up at her, anger slipping behind raw pain, it took all her restraint not to pull him into a hug and tell him ... what? *Try not to let the jerks of the world get to you.*

"Brian kissed her. Hard. Almost knocked her into the locker. She smacked him across the face and stormed off. The guys just stood there laughing. By the time I got close, Brian had his hands on his ears and was staring at his shoes." He turned fully to face his mother. "I couldn't believe they'd do that to someone who obviously couldn't defend himself, so I told Eddie to keep his stupid jokes to himself."

Annette could see the entire scene drawing out now. The same ageless scenario happened in schools everywhere since the dawn of time. "Who's going to make him?"

Adam nodded. "I got in his face and said I would."

"And he what? Shoved you? Hit you?"

"Something like that." Adam leaned back in his seat, facing forward. "I had to do it, Mom. I had to."

How could she tell her son that violence wasn't the answer when everything in her wanted to drive to this Eddie's house and knock some sense into his parents for raising a bully? "Your principal is right. Violence is never an answer."

And neither was sitting back and doing nothing.

Right now Annette would give anything for the days when all it took to make her kids stop hurting was to kiss the boo-boo. Unsure of where to start, she picked up the phone and called the one person most likely to have the answers.

A teacher at the local high school, Emily was another member of the Everrett clan. People Annette had come to count on since moving to Kona. "Hello?"

"Hey, Em. It's Annette Deluca."

"Gee, this is a nice surprise. What's up?"

"Honestly I'm looking for some answers."

"If I've got 'em, I'm willing to share."

Annette could hear Emily's smile through the phone. "Adam ran into a little trouble at school today."

"What kind of trouble?" A sharp edge instantly replaced her earlier easy tone.

"He got into a fight with a school bully."

"There is a lot of enlightenment on school bullying. I can recommend several sites for you to go to, if Adam is a target. They're—"

"No. He's not the target."

Emily didn't respond.

"He was defending another kid."

"Okay. That's a new excuse for fighting."

"I'm sorry to hear that."

"I don't mean to make it sound like there are never any children who stand up for the bullied. I just don't hear about it very often."

"Probably like the news. We hardly ever hear about the good deeds, but we hear all about the bad ones."

"I suppose. What do you need from me?"

"I want to help, but I don't know how. Adam says the boy is 'weird smart.'" Annette ran through the list of traits Adam had given her.

"I'm not an expert on this, but my first thought is the kid's on the autism spectrum. Most likely high functioning or he wouldn't be mainstreamed. And obviously very smart academically, but I'm guessing he doesn't really know what to do with that page of information he recited."

"I don't know."

"Any chance you can talk to the parents? Find out more about what's going on?"

"I thought about that, but I wanted to get some firsthand info."

"All I know is structure is crucial for these kids. They are each so different. It's not a disease, like diabetes, with a list of specific symptoms. There are red flags, but nothing is set in stone. If you've met one autistic child, you've met one autistic child. Think of it as meeting a five-foot-tall brown-haired boy with brown eyes and an IQ of 160. Nothing else about him will be the same as the next five-foot-tall brown-haired boy with brown eyes and a 160 IQ. Nor the next. That's part of what makes this such a challenging disorder. There are no rules. No standards. No two children will ever be exactly alike. It's a spectrum. A scale. The variations are limitless."

"What is the school doing for these kids?"

"Again, every child is different. Some more sensitive

than others. Literally. Depending on the situation a teacher or fellow student can be assigned to shadow the child. Follow them from a distance, make sure he doesn't get himself into difficulties he's incapable of escaping."

"Like a bully."

"Like a bully. Though you may want to thank your lucky stars if this boy is not on social media. Nowadays that's the larger threat. The name-calling and singling out of children in school carries over into social media at home. The victim has no escape. No safe haven. Parents don't often realize what is going on. Everyone grew up with expressions like 'sticks and stones may break my bones, but names will never hurt me.' But they do. And it's become even more vicious in recent years."

"So what do I do?"

"First you need to let the school know exactly what's been going on. Teachers can't help if they don't see the poor behavior and if the kids don't tell them. Then you should probably talk to the young boy's family. Find out if he is, indeed, autistic or if there's some other issue involved. After that, enlightening the parents of the bully would be a good idea. Sometimes these kids take after their parents. They're bullied or insecure at home. I hate to keep spitting clichés at you, but children learn what they see. On the other hand, I've known some of the nicest parents who did everything right and were completely aghast at what their son or daughter did to other children at school. Talking to the bullied boy's parents is the best way to move forward. At least then Adam and the school will know what they're up against." Emily paused. "And, off the record, Adam did good. I'm proud of him for standing up for what's right."

"I am too." Annette wished Tom could be here to see his son, already behaving like a man. After a few polite words about the weather and the upcoming winter break and its holiday dinners at Emily's mom's, Annette hung up with a new mission. Find and speak to Brian's parents.

CHAPTER THREE

A multitude of physicians and therapists through the years had told Michael and Karen that Brian's screen time needed to be held to a minimum if they wanted to improve his socialization skills. At an early age Brian could spend hours happily on a computer tablet, playing word and counting games far above his age level. When neighborhood children were babbling and interacting, but Brian remained focused in his own world, Karen knew something wasn't right.

Today, however, seemed to call for a bending of the rules and letting Brian indulge in soothing his mind with a favorite computer game. Deep down, Mike still hoped one day Brian would use that computerlike brain for something amazing, like finding a cure for cancer or world famine, but Mike would gladly settle for his son having a happy life. Mike's glance shifted to the photograph on his desk. When Karen had succumbed to a burst aneurysm, he'd clung to the good memories and pushed one foot in front of the other, expecting someday he wouldn't miss her so very much. "You always made it look so easy."

The sound of his cell chiming in his pocket had him setting down the beloved photo of Karen and Brian, and answering, "Becker."

"Hello, Mr. Becker. My name is Annette Deluca."

The name didn't ring any bells. Was she the homeroom monitor? Or whatever they called the mom who organized all the parents nowadays. "Hello."

"Am I catching you at a bad time?"

His gaze shot past his office door to the living room, where Brian smiled over his iPad. Was there ever a good time? "This is fine. How may I help you?"

"My son, Adam, got into a fight at school today."

Mike's spine stiffened. If this woman thought calling to apologize for her child's cruel behavior ...

"Normally I don't approve of violence as a response to a negative situation, but, as much as I think that other boy deserved a good throttle, I'd like to avoid putting our boys through this again."

Our boys? Karen's voice echoed in the back of his mind. *"Look at our boy, Mike. He's so smart."*

"I'm sorry." Mike shook his head in an effort to clear his mind. If this wasn't the bully's mother, then she must be ... "What exactly are we talking about?"

"Oh, excuse me. I thought you knew. My son, Adam, got in a fight with a bully at school for telling your son to kiss a girl."

Kiss a girl? His neighbor had only relayed what little information her daughter had shared with her after school. All he really knew was that Brian had been picked on again, and a boy from another class came to his defense. A girl would certainly be an easy button to push for Brian. Mike had so hoped mainstreaming here in Hawaii would be different. "I was planning to call the school about this first thing in the morning."

"I know it's short notice, but, if you have a few minutes, perhaps we could meet somewhere and discuss what happened."

"That won't really be necessary. I'm sure the school—"

"Mr. Becker, I'll be honest. This is the first difficult situation involving Adam that I've had to face on my own, and I would prefer to be better informed, before I decide how to deal with my son."

And how could he say no to a request like that? Hadn't he wished a hundred times in the last three years that he could have someone to talk to about Brian? "I can't leave Brian alone. Would you be willing to come to our home?"

"Of course."

For the next hour Mike did his best to finish up the work in front of him. Despite his mind's eagerness to veer off path and consider Annette Deluca, her son, and this new mess, the demands of Mike's job didn't allow him that luxury. By the time the doorbell rang, he'd pretty much given up on making any progress on either front.

Taking two seconds to glance into Brian's room and make sure he was settled in for the night, Mike proceeded to the front entryway and resisted the urge to straighten his collar.

At the other side of the door stood a dark-haired petite woman with big round eyes and a nervous smile. "Michael?"

"Yes." He stepped aside and extended a hand toward the living room. "Please come in."

"Thank you."

Mike did his best not to watch the shift of her hips. Why was he even looking? He had no interest in women. Not anymore.

Annette did her best not to fidget. There was no reason for her to be so nervous, but for some reason, her stomach was doing somersaults and back-springs. Michael Becker stood across from her by the armchair, and she wondered how long before his wife joined them.

"Would you like something to drink?"

"No, thank you." Where to begin? "Is your wife not home?"

The already grim expression on the man's face intensified. "No." He took a seat. "Karen's been gone for almost three years."

Gone? She didn't even want to contemplate what he meant. Today was difficult enough. "How much do you know about what happened at school this afternoon?"

"According to my neighbor's daughter, a boy named Eddie has been teasing my son."

She blew out a breath and bobbed her head. "I'd say it's more than just teasing. Eddie is apparently the class bully.

He likes to torment the not-so-popular, and now he's targeting your son."

Michael's lips thinned, and his brow creased.

"As I mentioned on the phone, my son, Adam, saw Eddie talk your son into kissing a girl. Adam was too late to stop it, but he fought the boy for making fun of Brian."

Michael's throat bobbed. "I only knew the gist of the situation before your call."

"I spent my afternoon in the principal's office." Annette wished she'd accepted his offer of a drink; it would have given her hands something to do. "I'd like to know more about Brian."

"He's autistic. High functioning. But socialization is not something that comes easy for him."

That lined up with what Emily had told her. "That possibility has been suggested."

Casually he leaned forward, his joined hands resting on his knees. "Do you know anyone on the autism spectrum?"

She shook her head.

"Brian's a sweet, warm, wonderful boy. And smart as a whip. But he doesn't understand normal social cues."

He blew out a deep sigh that Annette suspected represented more than a long day. She had a feeling she was listening to years of exhaustion and future anticipations all wrapped up in a single breath.

"Routine is very important," he continued. "As long as we don't change the familiar, he's a joy to be around."

For a moment she saw the gleam of a proud parent in his eyes.

"But I'll admit, I don't know what to do about this." His pleading eyes lifted and met hers. "Are you sure I can't get you something to drink? Juice? Coffee? Tea?"

"A cup of tea would be nice."

"Good." He pushed to his feet. "One cup of tea coming right up."

Her gaze followed his steps across the room. From where she sat, she could see Michael moving about the kitchen. He opened cabinet doors and pulled out cups, saucers. Next he tugged at the drawers and retrieved spoons.

A kettle simmered on the stove.

"Do you have a flavor preference?" He popped his head out the doorway.

Taking that as her cue to join him, she stood. "What are my choices?"

In the kitchen Michael held out a large tin of specialty teas. "I'm rather boring and always drink black tea. Karen liked fruity flavors."

Annette scanned the choices and pointed at the corner package. "I'm rather fond of Earl Grey."

"Earl Grey it is."

Easing farther into the room, she gestured toward the kitchen table. "Do you mind?"

"Make yourself at home."

Waiting for the kettle to boil, she slipped into the nearest chair. "My son and I have had a long talk."

Michael nodded.

"I've explained to him that violence is never the answer." The memory of her son's grin at giving Eddie a split lip made her smile. "I don't think he believes me completely."

The frown on Michael's face lifted, replaced by a lazy smile.

He had a nice smile.

"I don't think we ever truly get over the need to occasionally beat the sh ... to knock sense into someone who rightly deserves it."

"That may be, but punching everyone we think deserves it isn't the answer either."

Michael's smile slipped, and he shook his head. "No. No, it's not."

"I'll be talking with the school tomorrow, but Adam and I have come up with a plan of sorts."

"Really?" The kettle whistled, and he turned off the stove.

She nodded her head. "Adam wants to be Brian's study buddy. At least that's the name we've given it. If you agree, we could ask the school to transfer Brian into more classes with Adam."

"That could be a problem." He filled the cups. "Remember what I said about routine being important? Brian only needs to do something once for it to become the standard. By now he's gotten used to his teachers, the students. He probably knows how many steps there are between each classroom."

"Hmm. I didn't realize. The idea is for Adam to keep an eye on Brian."

"Milk or sugar?"

Annette shook her head.

Michael set the cup on the table and took a seat across from her. The way he gazed into the cup, as he dipped the teabag in and out, made her wish she could read minds.

"And," Annette continued, "Adam's hoping to uncover something they might have in common. A foundation of sorts for building a friendship."

"It would be nice for Brian to have a friend." He smiled.

She blew on the hot liquid. "That's what we thought."

"I'm just concerned the solution may be more difficult for him than the problem."

"I hope not." She took a brief sip. "Adam has given this a lot of thought. Does Brian like sports?"

"A little. Mostly it's keeping track of statistics. But, yes." Mike took a long moment to study her. "I am starting to believe Adam may be an answer to prayer."

"I hope so. I, on the other hand"—she bit back a smile—"he will be Eddie's worse nightmare."

CHAPTER FOUR

A rash of interruptions had filled Annette's morning. Early Christmas shopping had been taken off her to-do list, and if her phone rang one more time, she was going to throw the thing into the Pacific Ocean. Lunchtime for Adam and Brian started in a few minutes. Running late, she had just enough time to get her car into a parking space, hurry into the building, and sign in at the office.

The school's policy of allowing parents to lunch with their children made her plans much easier. As small children in elementary school, having Mom or Pop in for lunch was always seen as a big treat. Though few preteens held that same enthusiasm for their mothers eating lunch with them, under the circumstances, Adam was more than glad to have Annette tag along for a little while.

She'd barely set foot in the cafeteria when she spotted the first problem. The split-lip kid was making his way to the table where Adam, his friend Cory—who wanted to help too—and Brian were seated. Though he looked a little stiff, there was nothing that would have led her to believe that Brian was any different than any other boy in class. If she picked up her pace, she just might beat Eddie there. Maybe.

"Slumming Deluca?" The tough kid almost sneered.

Annette reached her son's table just in time to hear Split Lip's remark. "Eddie. How nice to see you. Will you be joining us for lunch?"

Mike wiped down clean countertops. He'd already emptied the trash in every room and hauled it out back. He'd also taken the microfiber mop and dusted the floors. It was his way of productively pacing until Annette came by after lunch to report. Not even Brian's first day of school had left Mike this nervous and unsettled.

Which begged a totally new question. Was it Brian's day or Annette's impending visit that had Mike prowling like an alley cat? Tensing in place, he looked up and out the window, taking in the driveway and steadily traveled street. The compromise for wanting an oceanfront home was having a main drag at his front door. Not that a main drag in a place like Kona was ever *that* busy. And letting his mind wander off about real estate didn't change the truth of why he was nervous.

He and Karen had been high school sweethearts. She'd graduated and gone on to Florida State; he'd ventured farther away and attended Stanford. By the end of his sophomore year, rather than grow apart, he'd concluded Karen was the only girl for him. And, thank the Lord, she'd decided the same thing. Graduation was in May and the wedding in June. He'd be a liar if he said he'd never noticed a pretty woman. After all, being married didn't mean he'd lost his eyesight. But none appealed to him. Not even after Karen's death. Well-intended friends had eventually introduced him to a parade of attractive women, who should have had any normal red-blooded American male eager to return to the dating game. But he still wasn't interested. Not even a little. Until now. This woman most definitely qualified as *interesting*.

A midsize SUV turned into his drive, and, eager to learn about the lunchtime experiment, he had to stop himself from running for the door. Curiosity won out over patience, and, instead of casually walking to the entryway, he trotted from the kitchen.

Pulling the door open wide, he waited until Annette was within earshot. "How did it go?"

"Good." She picked up her pace, until she reached the stoop. "Really good."

While his mind had been doing a song and dance only a few minutes ago about the subject of Annette, right now all he wanted to know about was his son. "I made lemonade. Why don't we grab a couple of glasses and head out to the lanai."

Annette dipped her chin in agreement and followed him to the kitchen. "First of all, I just want to say that, had I not known Brian was autistic, I'm not sure I would have figured it out on my own."

Mike handed her a glass and started toward the patio doors. "How is that?"

"Well, I think I would have labeled him as shy. Probably introverted too."

Mike couldn't argue with her. He and Karen had thought that same thing when Brian was a toddler.

"For instance, whenever Adam or Cory—"

"Cory?"

"Adam's best friend."

Best friend. Mike hadn't considered that Adam would have more friends who would want to get involved with Brian. Mike had just assumed Adam was some sort of do-good loner. Maybe one of the brainiacs.

"Anyhow, whenever the boys asked Brian a question, he'd look up and answer, like any other kid. Then I noticed that anytime Adam or Cory spoke to Brian, they always said his name first. I realized they wanted to make sure they had Brian's full attention."

Mike nodded. He often had to step in front of the computer or TV, if he wanted information from his son.

"And that's when I realized the methodical way Brian eats his food."

"It's all part of his routine. When he was little, his hotdogs had to have a squiggly line of mustard in just the right pattern, or he'd have a bit of a meltdown."

Annette's brow crinkled in thought.

She'd done that a few times last night while explaining her plan to him, and it looked just as cute on her this afternoon as it had yesterday.

"After everything you explained to me about the

importance of his routine, I was a bit concerned Brian was going to have a hard time at lunch with the three of us joining him. But I was really pleased."

Now Mike was able to blow out the last bit of breath trapped at the base of his lungs waiting for good news. For years he'd been told that, sometimes around puberty, situations improved for autistic children. Change would no longer be such a horrible thing. Reactions to breaks in routine less exhausting. He'd been hoping Brian would be one of those kids. Now he had a solid reason to believe this might just be the case for his son.

"Eddie, on the other hand, that kid is a real piece of work."

Mike's spine stiffened. He should have known something would go wrong.

"He is nothing but a big bully. My son warned me, and, brother, was he right."

"What did Eddie do?"

"To the boys, nothing. But when I invited him to join us at the table—"

"You invited him to what?"

"Oh." She shrugged. "When I reached the table, Eddie was all set to pick on Adam for who-knows-what, but he didn't quite know what to make of me showing up."

Not much made Mike want to smile nowadays, but picturing petite Annette making nice with a middle-school bully probably as tall as she was made him want to grin from ear to ear. "I think I would have liked to have seen that."

"It was quite the sight. The kid's eyes rounded like a pair of golf balls, and he shook his head so hard it might have been at risk of rolling off his shoulders. Somehow he managed to mumble no. My son and Cory quietly snickered to themselves. Brian's expression was unchanged."

"I'm not surprised. That's exactly the sort of thing that flies over his head."

"Of course." She nodded before continuing. "I brought takeout for Adam and Cory, as you told me changing Brian's lunch would not be a treat for him but more of an upset. We talked for a bit about the boys' morning, and, while they chatted with each other, I kept an eye on Eddie across the room. I just knew if the parent volunteers hadn't stopped him from tormenting kids before, having me in the cafeteria now wasn't going to change that. Sure enough, somewhere between the conversation of tonight's basketball game and history homework, I noticed Eddie paying way too much attention to the table of girls to his right.

"Marsha Fitzsimmons is a sweet girl. Definitely shy and quiet, and probably one of the most intelligent children in Adam's grade. She and her smart friends would be easy targets for a bully. Rather than wait for the inevitable, I excused myself from our table and circled my way around the room, coming up behind Eddie and his friends, so they wouldn't know I was still watching. As the girls rose from the table, Eddie's big sneakered foot inched its way farther away from his seat. If I didn't know firsthand how much tripping those girls would not only embarrass them but prick at their emotional well-being, I would have laughed at Eddie's lack of imagination."

"You were teased in school?" The sudden snap of anger at her disclosure surprised him.

"Not me. My daughter. She's very pretty and graceful now, but, at the boy's age she had braces and wore glasses and was smart."

"Making her the perfect target for bullies."

"Not bullies. Just mean girls. Every school has them. Like bullies, they're a fact of life. One I told my daughter to ignore. That it would pass."

"And you were right."

She nodded slowly, a tiny crease forming between her brows. "But she shouldn't have to put up with the hurt. I should have done something then. I think it will always bother me that I didn't."

He didn't quite know what to say to that. How to respond. Karen would have had the right words, but, saving him from saying the wrong thing, Annette shrugged and pulled up a smile, shook off the emotional moment, bringing them back to lunchtime today.

"I waited until Marsha was little more than two feet away from him, then I came around and slid into the space beside him. Even pushed his foot over with mine, before sitting. Just a subtle show that I knew what he was up to."

"What did he do?" Suddenly visions of a growling hormonal pubescent teen shoving back had Mike wishing that he could be the one to spend lunches with his son instead of Annette.

"Gaped like a landed trout." She chuckled. "I know I shouldn't find so much pleasure in putting the kid in his place, but it was really nice. Same thing when his pimply-faced friend laughed at him. I moved over and sat next to the snickering kid. I'd have sidled up to every kid at the table, if they'd continued making fun of their own friends. When I informed them that I'd see them tomorrow, they all looked absolutely horrified."

"So, in an odd sort of way, you stood up for Eddie too."

That cute little frown was back. "I hadn't thought of it that way. But someone has to teach these kids to treat each other with respect."

Mike set his drink on the small glass table beside him on the lanai. "It'll take more than a lunch or two to retrain bullies."

"I'm not convinced they're that bad. Thoughtless, yes. A little cruel, maybe. But mostly I suspect their bad behavior is overcompensation. Time will tell. And I've got all year, if that's what it takes."

"I can't ask that of you."

"You're not. I want to do this. Besides, even if Eddie can't be truly reformed, I doubt it will take more than a few lunch visits to at least curb his behavior with Brian." She glanced away from Mike and turned her attention from one side of the sweeping windows to the other, taking in the broad view as though just now noticing they were on the ocean. "This is lovely."

"Thank you. Growing up in Florida, I've always loved the water. I've been blessed with a good career, even if it does eat up most of my waking hours. At least I can provide a good home for my family ... my son."

Her expression softened. "You mentioned your wife has been gone … was it three years?"

"Yes." Even after all this time, the too-familiar taste of hurt and anger swilled around his words. "I left for work in the morning the same way I did every day. Around noon I got a phone call from the police. Karen had been battling a headache the night before, and it hadn't gone away by breakfast. She'd collapsed at the grocery store. Aneurysm."

"I'm so sorry." Her hand lifted to him. Then halfway there, she snapped it back to her side.

An odd pang of loss kicked at him. It made no sense. He'd just met this woman and had no idea how comforting her touch could or would be, and yet he really wished she'd not pulled back. "Are you in a hurry?"

With a question in her eyes, she slowly shook her head.

"Up for a walk?"

"Don't you have to work?"

"The servers went down about ten minutes ago for maintenance." Living in a different time zone from the teams stuck running backups in the middle of the night did have its perks.

A smile took over her face. "I love walking on the beach. It's more fun with company."

Funny, he'd always thought that too.

CHAPTER FIVE

The closer to the shoreline Annette got, the more the softer black Kona sand shifted beneath her shoes. Not caring about being polite or proper, she leaned over and slid her foot out of one sandal, then the other. This was Hawaii after all, Hang Loose country.

In a pair of well-worn deck shoes, Michael Becker fell in step beside her, seemingly unconcerned with the sand. "In the months we've lived here, I'm still surprised to step outside and not see bright white sand."

Southern California had plenty of shoreline, but nothing she'd describe as bright or white. Except maybe Carmel. "Where did you used to live?"

"Florida. Key Biscayne."

"Aah. Land of the Eastern Retiree. How do they refer to it? … Oh, yeah. Southern Brooklyn."

Michael chuckled. "Some places do feel more like New York than Florida."

"Do you miss it?"

"Not really." Studying the horizon, he let a lazy smile appear. "Maybe a good Cuban sandwich. Or a conch fritter."

"Conch fritter. Didn't realize they were that easy to find north of the Florida Keys."

"Oh, yeah. They're all over south Florida, but the best are found in Key West."

"You get to Key West often?"

"It was a favorite vacation spot. No tedious plane rides for Brian but the feel of a distant trip." He turned to glance at her and smiled. "As long as you like the bohemian tourist feel."

"There is that." She liked his smile but got the impression he didn't do it often.

"Which part is most appealing? Bohemia or wall-to-wall tourists?"

She weaved close enough to the water for the foamy edges to wash over her toes. "Can I vote for conch fritters?"

"Absolutely." His gaze settled on some distant point. "What happened to Adam's father?"

The familiar sense of loss pricked her chest. Though less forcefully now. The often-asked question no longer carried the emotional impact of even a few short months ago. "A plane crash." From the corner of her eye she thought she saw Mike wince.

"I know the words don't help, but I am sorry for your loss." He slipped his hands into his pockets. "They say it gets easier."

"It's been almost two years. I'm still waiting."

He nodded.

She knew there wasn't much he could say. And she certainly didn't want this to turn into a pity party. "I'd like to hear what Brian has to say about today. Will you call me and let me know?"

"I will, but I can do better than that. Wednesday is pizza night. We eat at Carlo's. Why don't you and Adam join us for dinner?"

An unexpected jolt of raw excitement took her by surprise. "I'll check with Adam and Bethany."

Michael slowed his pace. "Bethany?"

"My daughter. Who, if I'm not mistaken, is going to explain to me in dramatic detail why having dinner with her younger brother and his new friend is not the way she wants to spend her evening."

"Oh, well. I certainly—"

"No, no. Hear me out." She raised her hand at him. "The excruciatingly long dissertation will most likely be followed by a surprisingly brief outline of appropriate plans for her that will undoubtedly not include her mother or her brother."

From the confused expression on Michael's face,

Annette was willing to bet the guy didn't have any sisters.

"Too much information?" she asked.

"No. Sorry. I'd always thought it would have been nice if Karen and I had had more children, but now"—a sly smile teased at one side of his mouth—"maybe Mother Nature knew better."

"Maybe I'm as guilty as my daughter of overdramatization. I can't imagine life without her. She's a really great young woman."

"I'm sure she is." Michael nodded, lifted his wrist and, glancing off to his left, then his right, he turned. "We should start back. I didn't realize how far we'd walked."

Annette wasn't completely sure where they were, but she couldn't see his house anymore. "Wow. Good plan." She remained on the side by the water's edge. It had been a while since she'd taken the time to walk the shore. Too long.

"Have you always lived in Hawaii?" Michael asked.

"Almost two years. This is an easier place to raise a family than L.A."

"That's what I thought." He hefted one shoulder in a casual shrug. "Not about L.A., but easier than the Miami area."

"How's it working out for you?"

Michael smiled down at her. "Better now."

And darned if that twinge of raw excitement didn't stir again. Was he flirting with her? Or was she reading too much into the single comment? After all, who wouldn't be better living in Kona? *Of course.* That was it. Life was simply better in Hawaii. Besides, if he were flirting, what in heaven's name would she do about it?

Keeping his hands in his pockets was the only way Mike could think of to stop from reaching out and touching Annette. The urge to hold her hand and kick through the waves with her was growing stronger with every step. When the words "plane crash" had slipped from her lips, the only thing he could think of was pulling her against him and cocooning her in his arms to keep her safe from any more hurt. Not that he could protect her or anyone else from the challenges life dished out. He'd tried that, and it hadn't worked out so well. So he shoved his hands into his pockets and kept them there.

The truth of the matter was he didn't come close to understanding what was going on at the moment. Quite frankly he didn't trust himself. Was he attracted to Annette Deluca because she was a beautiful, smart, funny, sensitive woman? Or was he just infatuated with the only person who had stepped up to protect and help his son in ways he couldn't? He might have been able to carve out an hour or so of time to evaluate his son's circumstances, but there was no way he could make lunchtime at school part of his everyday routine. And he certainly wouldn't have infused himself into Eddie the bully's space.

He swallowed a laugh. This woman might have been physically petite, but she was proving to be a real pistol. Which made him want to get to know her better. Much better. Not that he could get too close. He honestly didn't think he was up to a relationship, and, even if by some strange chance he were, Annette had lost her husband less than two years ago. From the way her gaze softened with every mention of Mr. Annette Deluca, he'd be willing to bet a year's salary that she was a woman who had been very much in love with her husband. The lucky guy.

"My neighbor, Liz, owns a boutique in town. Her daughter is a year ahead of Brian, so it was pretty convenient for her to pick up both kids. She's been terrific about Brian's idiosyncrasies. Without fail Liz picks up both kids at exactly the same time every day. We lead a very routine life. On Wednesdays we leave for dinner at exactly five thirty. I park in the far corner of the lot, where I can always find a space quickly. The manager figured out, after only a few weeks, that Brian was a creature of habit, and now he reserves the same table for us."

"That's very nice of him."

He nodded. "I'd hoped life in a smaller, more relaxed town would be easier for us, but I never anticipated just how friendly everyone would be. It's been an unexpected blessing." Finding a support circle to match what his wife had developed in Florida had been a major concern for him and one of the biggest negatives to this entire move. Now he felt rather foolish for ever having worried. "If you don't mind, it will be easier on Brian if you would meet us at the restaurant."

Nodding, she gave him a sweet smile. Not a polite one but sincere reassurance. "That will be just fine."

Just ahead he could see the cluster of houses, announcing their return. A small part of him wished they could ignore his house and keep walking. "And here we are."

Single file they turned into his yard, then into his house. Neither said a word, an easy silence nestling around them. At the front door he faced Annette, his hands still safely in his pockets. "Thank you again."

"My pleasure. Really."

Having a purpose, he dared to bring his right hand out in the open and reached for the doorknob. Stepping aside, he held open the door. "See you tonight."

"Five thirty." Still smiling, she wiggled her fingers in a cute good-bye wave.

He kept an eye on her until her car backed out of the driveway and disappeared down the road. Five thirty couldn't come fast enough.

Billy Everrett looked up from behind his desk at the dive shop. "Annette. What a nice surprise." He pushed to his feet.

"Don't get up on my account." She gestured for him to retake his seat. "I was on my way home and had an idea I wanted to follow through with you."

"Shoot." Despite her waving him off, Billy remained

standing until she'd taken a seat. She didn't know if it was his military training or Maile Everrett's upbringing, but Billy never ceased to amaze her. The same could be said for Nick, Doug, and the other fellows she'd met through the dive shop. Maybe the answer wasn't one or the other but a little of both.

"I've recently come to know a young autistic boy."

"The one you spoke to Emily about?"

Annette nodded. "Word sure gets around fast."

"It's a small island." Billy smiled. "And you got my sister thinking too."

"I did?"

He bobbed his head. "Yes, but let's see what you have on your mind first."

"I know you guys work with wounded warriors. Do special group dives, efforts to help with PTSD, and other issues."

Billy nodded again.

"Do you think you could develop some sort of program for autistic kids?"

The way Billy's eyes widened, she had a feeling whatever she'd said hadn't been a good idea.

"I don't know enough about it, but I'm not sure thirty feet underwater is a good place to find out if it's a bad idea." Leaning over his desk, he folded his hands. "Maybe something in the dive pool might work though. I'd have to do some research. And talk to my sister."

"Fair enough." She hoped something could be done. Adam loved anything to do with the water, and sharing that with Brian could be another bridge for the young man. "What did Emily have to say?"

"Not very much. We were at Mom's for dinner last night. At some point the conversation came around to her students this year and your conversation about a new boy at the junior high." He snapped his fingers. "Which reminds me. Mom wants you to find out what the boy's favorite cookies are."

Annette almost laughed out loud. The only thing surprising about Billy's comment was that Maile hadn't already found out the answer for herself. That woman had a way of knowing everything. "I'll see what I can do. Now, you were saying?"

"At the mention of possible autism, Doug asked if there were any sports programs in the school district for special needs children."

"Like Special Olympics?"

"Maybe. But I think he was referring to smaller school programs. Emily was going to get more info on one of the high school programs."

And from what Annette had learned about the Everrett family and their friends, if there was a way for them to be involved, they soon would be. Her heart still swelled with appreciation when she thought back to the time after the plane crash. Trapped in a broken body in a Los Angeles intensive care unit, she could not care for her children. Never mind uncover the true cause of the plane crash that killed her husband and almost killed her.

But Billy and his friends had quickly learned that the crash had been no accident. And, more importantly, that Adam and Bethany could be in danger. Doug, Jim, and the others from Billy's former EOD team had come running when Billy said he needed help protecting her children and Maggie, the woman who had been more like family than a mere household manager. Heck, Jim had come days before his wedding, ticking off his then fiancée. Annette bit back a smile. Yep, if the closest thing to *family* she had here got involved in the special needs community, Michael and Brian Becker were about to learn that moving to Kona was the best thing to happen to them since Maile Everrett's coconut fritters.

CHAPTER SIX

One of the nice things about Carlo's was that, in a large nook at the back of the restaurant, the owners had installed a game area to entertain the children as their parents finished their meals. The first time Mike had noticed that section, he'd been concerned the noise would be off-putting to his son, but, focusing on his game of choice, Brian was almost oblivious to all the sounds surrounding him. "I have to admit, I'm surprised."

Annette swallowed her last bite of pizza. "At what?"

"How easy tonight has turned out."

"In what way?"

"When Brian was a baby, my wife arranged playdates. Mostly mother-and-toddler events. As he grew older, it became more challenging."

"I can imagine."

He bit back the urge to ask, *Can you*? In less than a day it was impossible for a bystander to understand the ordinary challenges faced by the parent of an autistic child. For years he'd lived in the same house with an autistic child and not until Karen died had he discovered just how much he hadn't realized. "I could be reading this wrong, but it looks like Brian and Adam are friends."

Her face lit up. "You're not. They are. So what did Brian have to say about school?"

"More than I expected. Nothing terribly revealing. Social cognition is not my son's strength. He takes everything at face value. No room for nuance or socially understood undertones. But I know that Brian is in class with Adam and that Adam likes school. Adam is friends with Cory. Adam is five foot two inches. Brian mentioned that several times. I suspect that might have something to do with how Adam likes to play basketball."

"Adam likes to scuba dive too."

"Okay, it might be totally uncool of me, but the picture brewing in my mind scares the bejeesus out of me. And I was raised in the water."

"Never dived?"

"Oh, I have. Which is why the idea of my twelve-year-old son doing it is so frightening."

Covering her mouth with her hand, Annette did her best to mask her laughter. Especially since this time he was pretty sure she was laughing at him, not with him. "It's pretty tame at Adam's age. And plenty of years of snorkeling came first. The Big Island Dive shop has a training pool and lots of classes for young kids. They're a great group of people."

"Do you dive?"

Annette beamed. "You bet. I love the water. It's why we bought a vacation home here."

"Vacation? But Adam's in school."

Her gaze dropped to the table. "After I got out of the hospital—"

"The hospital?"

The way she drew in a deep ragged breath, Mike wished he had kept his stupid mouth shut.

"I was also in the plane crash. My husband and the pilot were killed instantly. I spent a great deal of time in intensive care. When I finally was released and able to travel, I joined my children here to finish my rehab."

Intensive care? Rehab? He'd quickly learned she had the tenacity of a pit bull, but that didn't begin to describe the strength this woman must draw upon. Mike took a good long look. Not just at the surface: the pretty eyes, sweet smile, silky hair, or the hint of cleavage that could easily feed his imagination for hours—if he let it run in that direction. Instead he focused on how she held her shoulders straight, erect, proud. Her chin high, firm, strong. And her eyes. Almost caramel in color with flecks of yellow shone with compassion and warmth. The same qualities that had no doubt pushed her to stand up for Brian in the first place.

"The kids were settled in school already," she continued, "and Los Angeles didn't appeal anymore. The smog. The traffic. The flash. The attitude. I couldn't deal with it. I needed … simple. So here we are."

"You're amazing."

Her cheeks turned several shades of pretty pink. Big eyes looked up at him through long lashes. He was in some serious trouble.

Lunchtime the last few days had gone about the same. Annette brought Adam and Cory takeout, while Brian ate his regular fare. Eddie had veered too close to a table of "uncool" kids, but, when he caught sight of Annette watching him, he'd cut a wider path. She would have to figure out a long-lasting way to deal with this kid after she no longer came to lunch. A few more kids had joined her son's table. The original group of three now consisted of six. All thoughtful of Brian. Annette noticed that, on occasion, when too many of the kids were all horsing around at the same time, Brian seemed to pull into himself, but she had yet to notice any of the meltdowns that Mike had warned her of. She had to wonder if maybe Brian's desire to be mainstreamed went hand in hand with a growing ability to manage the world around him. For his sake she certainly hoped so.

"There you are."

Annette looked up to see Emily Everrett approach their lunch table.

"Hey. What are you doing here?"

"Looking for you. You're not answering your phone."

Annette gave an apologetic wince. "I turn it to Silent while we're at lunch."

"That's what Maggie said."

"You called Maggie?" Boy Emily must really want to talk to her. Unless … Her heart lurched and lodged in her throat, almost robbing her of air. "Is something wrong with Bethany?"

"No, no." Emily shooed her over and sat beside her. "This is about a new program. I'm meeting with the principal in thirty minutes and thought you might want to join me."

"Me? Why me?"

"It would be good to have some parental backup."

"Ah. A blood sacrifice."

Emily laughed. "Maybe not that bad. But I wouldn't mind if you sat in."

"Does this have something to do with Brian?"

"It does."

"Then the one who should sit in is Mike. Not me."

"*Mike*?" Emily batted her eyes at her friend. "Not *Michael* or *Mr. Becker*?"

Annette shook her head and rolled her eyes upward. "You've been spending too much time in high school."

"Okay, okay. And I agree about Brian's father, but he can't break away."

"You asked him?"

"Of course I did. This is official school business. I do have access to parent records."

"But you teach at the high school, not the junior high."

"Doesn't matter. Same district. Besides, this is Kona not New York City."

Annette shrugged. "So what have you got on your mind?"

"At dinner the other night, Doug asked about school sports programs. I remembered that, last year, the high school started a unified basketball program. I checked around and turns out it's been a huge success. Each of the district's unified teams consists of three special needs players and two regular students. This way the special needs children feel a part of things, and the other kids, who maybe aren't talented enough to play on the varsity teams, feel better about themselves as well. Gives everyone a chance to shine a bit. A real self-esteem booster. It's working better than the district had hoped. I'm thinking the program could be beneficial at the junior high level. I looked into it, and I think there are enough special education students for the concept to work, but we'd have to move fast if they're going to start alongside the regular season."

"Adam does love to play but didn't think he was good enough to try out for the school team."

"See what I mean?" Emily's dimples bookended her bright smile. "You're the perfect person to help convince the principal that this will be a good experiment."

The bell rang, signaling the end of lunch. Annette scanned the room, looking for Eddie and his friends. Something in her gut told her to follow the kids as they shoved their lunch remnants into a bag, gathered their things, and filed out of the cafeteria. "I'm going to tag along here a minute, and then I'll meet you at the principal's office."

"No problem. I've got a few minutes. I'll be right behind you."

Sure enough, at the end of the hall, Eddie and his band of troublemakers huddled in wait. Annette shook her head and, instead of merely shadowing the boys, picked up speed and zipped ahead of them, stopping short in front of Eddie. "How are you today?" she asked the startled tween.

"Uh …"

"Have you met my friend Ms. Everrett? She's the math teacher at the high school."

Somehow the kid's eyes grew even rounder.

Emily extended her hand. "Nice to meet you."

"Hello." He looked down at her hand, as though it were capable of biting off his arm, but finally reached out to shake.

"I'm also in charge of the theater arts productions, so, if you think you'd enjoy being in the plays or working on the stage crew, I'm the person to see."

For a split second Annette thought she saw a twinkle in the kid's eye. Did the kid want to act, sing, or build a fake world? Another challenge. Emily's earlier words about building self-esteem in the regular students started an idea percolating. "Do you by any chance play basketball, Eddie?"

"No, ma'am. I mean, not on the school team."
"But you like to play?"
Eddie kicked his toe into the vinyl floor. "Some."
Glancing sideways, Annette caught Emily's satisfied nod. Things were definitely looking up.

CHAPTER SEVEN

Mike couldn't believe it. Brian was actually doing homework, and peace still reigned. He had no idea how Adam had pulled it off, but the two kids sat at the kitchen table like any pair of average schoolkids anywhere in the world. No drama. No strained nerves. Just focused work.

According to the clock on the wall, Annette would be here any minute to pick up Adam. Every day for over a week she'd called to report how the school day had gone, and then she'd listen patiently for Mike to replay Brian's perception of the day. Most times Brian had little to say, but that was okay. Everything had become routine for him. Routine was good.

Bit by bit they'd continued chatting past talk of the boys. And tonight he was looking forward to a little face-to-face conversation. At least he hoped she and Adam wouldn't have to rush off.

In the last ten minutes, he'd changed his shirt—twice—stopped to look in the mirror to ensure he hadn't sprouted a third eye or a stray cowlick—three times—and decided there was no need to straighten the living room—again. If the doorbell hadn't finally rung, who knows what ridiculous distraction he'd have fallen for.

"Hi." He opened the door wide. "The boys are still working. Are you in a hurry?"

She crossed the threshold. "Not at all."

"Good." He waved her in. "Would you like something cold to drink, or I could put the kettle on for tea?"

"Tea would be great."

"Earl Grey?"

"Yes." Her smile grew a little wider. "Thanks."

"Have a seat on the sofa and I'll be right back."

Bobbing her head, Annette sat on the oversize sofa and resisted the urge to wipe her hands on her slacks. Maybe she should have worn the khaki skirt. She'd only changed three—or was it four?—maybe five times before settling on white slacks and a simple lavender cotton top. As nervous as she was, anyone would think she was a teenager crushing on the captain of the football team.

Though how many high school crushes had their teenage children for chaperones? That thought had her chuckling. She was being ridiculous, and she knew it, but she'd forgotten the giddy excitement that came from liking a guy and getting to know him better and even daydreaming about the possibilities. Heck, when she'd met Tom, she actually had been a teenager. She never expected to feel this way again. Ever. And she most definitely liked it.

"Here you go." Mike set the mug in front of her.

He remembered she didn't use milk or sugar, which made her want to smile again. "Thanks."

"Hope you don't mind I nuked the water instead of using a kettle."

"Not a problem. If my life depended on it, I'm not sure I could find a kettle in my kitchen."

Mike settled in a chair in front of her. A mug in one hand, his other hand came to rest atop the ankle he had just crossed over his thigh. The casual pose looked to be the perfect magazine cover shot. She wished she had a camera and the liberty to capture the moment. Searching for words, Annette stalled, blowing on the warm liquid. "Did Emily tell you the school is making the junior high unified basketball teams a priority?"

"The boys have been talking about it. Adam is so patient. Brian gets one thought in his mind and tends to repeat it frequently throughout the conversation, and Adam simply answers and keeps going."

"Well, normally any program like this would take more than a couple of weeks to organize and implement, but so many people have come together to make this happen fast.

The first practice is already scheduled for next week. Nick and Billy from the Big Island Dive shop have offered to supply the uniforms. Doug, one of the dive instructors and Emily's fiancé, has volunteered to coach our team with Mr. Gatlin, the science teacher."

"That's very nice of the dive shop."

"They're very nice people."

"Sounds like it. But from the few conversations I've had with Gatlin, I wouldn't have expected him to be a sports fan."

"He's not." Annette bit back a smile. "That's why Doug is the assistant coach. The district requires a certified teacher be the head coach. Mr. Gatlin doesn't know a blessed thing about basketball, but he does believe in the program, so he stepped up. Next year, when the regular PE teacher is back from maternity leave, she'll take over coaching."

"I gather she's the sports fan."

"More than that, she went through college on a basketball scholarship. She's so excited she's threatening to get up from bed rest to come watch the games." Mike's brow crinkled into a concerned frown, so Annette answered the unasked question. "She's having twins, and the doctor wants her off her feet for the last six weeks of her pregnancy."

His forehead smoothed, and he shook his head. "I can't imagine raising twins. Karen and I were challenged with one. When Brian was a baby, we'd worry because he wouldn't nap. Then we'd worry if he napped too long." He chuckled. "Looking back, I realize we were a bit hyper-concerned."

"Not unusual for first-time parents. I spent a lot of hours watching Bethany sleep, mostly to make sure she was still breathing."

The two chuckled more loudly.

Mike scrubbed the smile from his face. "Considering how frightening it is being responsible for a tiny person, it's amazing that anyone has more than one."

"Oh, but they're so precious."

"They are," he agreed. "Did you ever consider having more?"

"Actually I did. But a friend of ours told me the problem with three children is you're always one arm or one parent short. The advice made sense, so I settled for two. Though now, on days when I have too much time on my hands, I think it would be nice to have a little one around the house. Then I remember how much work raising toddlers is and think *maybe not*."

Mike took a sip of his tea. "You know what they say. *Small children, small problems. Big children, big problems*."

His gaze fell to the mug cradled in his hands, and, for the first time, Annette considered the weight Mike had to carry, worrying about his son's future, his old age after she and Mike weren't here to watch out for him anymore. ... *She and Mike.* Where had that come from? She didn't have any responsibility for Brian. At least none that would continue much longer. Things had settled at school. Eddie and his crew were laying low. That might change, once she no longer joined the kids for lunch, but maybe things would be okay. Especially with Eddie participating in the new basketball program. Hopefully with all their efforts Eddie and others would come to understand bullying of any kind was not appropriate or acceptable behavior.

Adam came from the kitchen. "Hi, Mom. We're about finished. I'm going to the bathroom, and then we can go."

She smiled and nodded and wished for a little more time with Mike. The conversation wasn't earth shattering. They weren't about to solve the problems of world peace or poverty, but it was *nice* just knowing Mike was here. Someone to talk to, if she wanted to, or to just *be*.

Sliding his ankle off his other leg, Mike set both feet on the ground and leaned forward in his chair. "I was thinking. Would you like to join me for dinner? Maybe catch a movie?"

Annette blinked. Was he talking about just the two of them? A date? A real date? Or was her own wishful thinking misinterpreting again? Did he mean her and the boys?

"Just the two of us," he added, as though he were reading her thoughts.

She almost laughed. The notion that anyone could read her mind should have scared the daylights out of her, but, instead, the idea made her a little warm all over. "I'd love to."

CHAPTER EIGHT

Never had a week seemed so long. Mike had no idea how the sitter was going to work out at nighttime, but he hoped that Brian's familiarity with their neighbor Liz would make her presence in their house less stressful for him. Just in case, they'd done a short test run of sorts. A few days ago Liz came over and stayed with Brian while Mike ran to the grocery store for an hour or so. When he'd returned, all was well. The shift to a new person keeping Brian company had been easy. Mike didn't understand if this had anything to do with the puberty theory, but, even though Brian still needed routine—a precise routine—his reactions when things veered off course seemed less dramatic. Mike wasn't fooling himself into thinking that Brian's fixated tendencies would simply go away, but, for whatever reasons, change was at least a little easier for his son to handle. And *that* was a good thing.

The address Annette had given him was in a more secluded neighborhood. And more affluent. Not that he was surprised by that. It hadn't taken him long to realize Annette was a stay-at-home mom, with a full-time household manager-slash-nanny, depending on what kind of help was needed. Any widow with that kind of resources wasn't likely to be living in a trailer park, and yet he was still a little surprised, and even awed, at the massive modern home at the top of the long drive. He was no slouch in the income department. Karen had been a stay-at-home mom, and they had still managed to live a very comfortable life and to build a nice nest egg for Brian's future. But there was no way he and Annette would have ever traveled in the same circles anyplace but here in Paradise.

Swallowing hard, he shook his mind clear. Tonight wasn't a social-economic forum; it was dinner. With a nice lady. A very nice lady. One he wanted to get to know better. Much better.

Every time he considered how far under his skin Annette Deluca had settled in, it surprised the heck out of him. Lots of people had said time would heal all wounds. He'd fall in love again. Live a full and happy life. And with each passing year he'd been more convinced every one of those Pollyannas were full of it. Until now. *Until now.* Where Annette's house had failed to intimidate him, the emotions surging inside him—at the realization that he was fully capable of falling in love with Annette Deluca—were almost enough to send him running home to Florida. To the familiar, the cold, and the empty. *Almost.* Instead he prayed he'd made the right choices for tonight. He desperately did not want their first date to be their last.

Parking the car in front of the massive entryway, Mike sucked in a deep breath, grabbed the small bouquet of fresh blooms, and hoped, once again, that he didn't look too lame bringing flowers. The wide-eyed look of surprise, followed by a sprawling grin on Annette's face as she opened the door and spotted the floral bouquet, told him he'd hit the mark. So far, so good.

"Oh, Mike. You shouldn't have." She whisked the flowers into her hands. "If you'll give me a couple of minutes, I'll get these in water."

He followed her into the house and marveled at the expansive layout. Then he froze at the view. Holy cow. From her perch on a hill, spectacular was too boring a word for the sight before him. *Wow.*

Having set the vase of fresh flowers on the coffee table, she sidled up beside him. "Beautiful, isn't it?"

"Impressive."

"It's why we bought the place. It was way more house than either of us had wanted, but we couldn't resist basking in that view every day."

"I can certainly understand why." Shaking away his nerves for the umpteenth time tonight, he turned to her.

"Shall we go?"

"Absolutely."

He waited for her to close and lock the front door. "Hope you're hungry."

"Starved."

Holding open the car door for her, Mike waited as she eased into the passenger seat. The leg of her capris shifted higher, and he took an extra second to admire the curve of her leg sliding in place. For the first time he noticed a slim scar snaking up the side of her calf, reminding him of the physical hell she'd been through. Which only made him want this incredible woman to be a big part of his life, even more than he had five minutes ago.

It was all Annette could do not to fidget during the drive to the restaurant. By the time they'd reached the end of town, all her anxiousness about this evening had smoothed away. Talking with Mike was fun and easy. She shouldn't have let herself get all worked up. So what if she hadn't been on a date in decades?

She'd spent most of the day wondering what he had in mind. Especially after he'd called and told her to dress comfortably. Not that there was much call for dressing up in Kona, but his being thoughtful enough to give her a heads-up said so much about the kind of man Mike Becker was. And she was so excited to get to know him better.

"Here we are." Mike pulled into the tiny parking lot of a white frame house tucked off the main road behind a wide band of trees and shrubs covered in twinkling multicolored holiday lights.

The tiny restaurant was so well hidden from view that Annette had never noticed it was here. "This looks adorable."

"My neighbor recommended its home cooking."

"Really?"

"You mentioned how much you enjoyed Maile

Everrett's culinary skills, so I thought, well, … if you don't like it, we can always go somewhere else." He climbed out of the car and circled quickly around to open her door.

"No. I think this is going to be perfect."

He extended his hand to help her out but managed to close her door and turn toward the weathered white building without letting go. Halfway to the restaurant door, his step slowed, and he glanced down at their joined hands, then up to her face. He seemed as surprised to notice he was still holding on as she'd been to have him not release his grip as soon as she'd exited the car. He lifted their hands slightly. "Is this okay?"

The gentle, innocent question shot her with a rush of adrenaline that nearly melted her heart. All she could do was nod.

His questioning gaze shifted to a bright smile, as his fingers threaded with hers. She felt lighter than she'd felt in ages. And liked it.

Mike did all the right things for a first date. Opened doors and pulled out chairs. When she rose to go to the ladies' room, he stood as well. When she came back, he stood again. His mama had definitely raised him right.

"This is absolutely fabulous." The mussels in white wine sauce had been superb, and now the coconut-crusted tilapia melted in her mouth. "Don't say anything to Maile, but I think this may be better than hers."

"My lips are sealed." He grinned.

For dessert they shared a fantastic pumpkin custard. Somehow mid dip the spoons momentarily clashed, then tangled. The dueling spoons came within seconds of sending dark custard flying across the room. Only unsteady hands from fits of laughter spared the neighboring diners the surprise of being doused in dessert.

Had Mike suggested they spend the entire evening chatting at the small table, she would have gladly agreed. As much as she'd hated to leave the tiny oasis from the ordinary world, once settled in the car, anticipation for the rest of the night rushed through her veins. "Where to now?"

"That's a bit of a surprise." Mike shifted gears and

pulled out of the parking lot. "And like dinner, if it's not to your liking, we can—"

"Go somewhere else," she finished for him. "I'm sure whatever you have planned is going to be great."

"We'll see." He flashed a sparkling smile, and Annette resisted the urge to stretch out her arm and snatch his hand in hers.

Not far down the main road, Mike turned inland a few blocks and pulled into the parking lot for the Funtime Bowling Lanes. After the sweet dinner, she wasn't quite sure what to make of this.

Mike lifted the console between them and pulled out a fresh pack of women's tennis socks and grinned, his smile less sure than a few minutes before. "You game?"

The little-boy look in his eyes had her ready and willing to do just about anything he asked. "Absolutely. Just don't hold it against me that I haven't held a bowling ball since I was twelve."

"Good. Then I won't look so bad when you realize I haven't bowled since I was in high school."

Once again he took her hand and didn't let go until they received their shoes at the counter. The majority of the bowlers occupied the lanes to the left of the establishment. Their assigned lane had them isolated to the far right. Which would explain the muffled conversation between Mike and the clerk, while Annette tested the fit of her rented shoes.

"Boy, things sure have changed since I was twelve." No more paper score sheets. As a matter of fact there was no need for scorekeeping of any kind. A large screen above kept track of pins for anyone and everyone to see. "I guess this makes it harder to cheat."

"I wouldn't have done that anyhow." Mike tied his shoelaces.

Annette pushed to her feet. "I was referring to me."

Mike chimed in laughing, and together they sifted through the various colored balls. Of course he chose one of the heavier black balls; she opted for an eight-pound purple. When she caught him looking oddly at her choice, she shrugged a shoulder. "It's my favorite color."

The way he nodded and walked away, she got the feeling that, along with her preferred choice of tea and love for Maile's cooking, her favorite color had just been filed away for future use. Her heart gave an extra kick, and her pulse took off at a fast clip. What was this man doing to her?

CHAPTER NINE

Midway through the game, Mike couldn't stop smiling. On the way to the bowling alley, he'd taken a minute to call Liz. Thankfully all was smooth sailing, and he'd been able to relax and just enjoy some fun time with Annette. Not that either of them were ready for a pro bowling tour, but, if there was a Cutest Butt Wiggle competition, Annette would be a champ. The way she scurried forward and flung the ball down the lane had been the best entertainment he'd had in so very long.

Whether it was one pin or ten, every time she actually knocked something down, they laughed, slapped high fives, hip checked, and the one time she actually got a strike, she threw her arms around him in a back-crushing squeeze. One he almost didn't let go from.

"Your turn." Annette beamed, walking past him, wiping her hands on a small bag of chalk. "We should do this with the kids. I bet they'd love it. Probably would beat me, but they'd have a blast."

Mike nodded, but his smile almost slipped. He couldn't imagine Brian handling the constant sounds and movement. His already hypersensitive nature would be on full-blast overload. Then again, so much had changed in the few weeks since Annette and Adam decided to get involved.

"What's wrong?" Annette dropped the bag on the ball return and moved in closer. "Your mouth is smiling, but your eyes aren't."

Did she know him that well already?

"Oh, my God. Of course. The noise. Brian wouldn't like the noise." Her hand flew to her mouth, and her brow crinkled in concern. "I'm so sorry," she mumbled through her fingers.

"Hey"—he closed the small gap between them—"don't feel bad. Few people understand the challenges Brian faces. At least you're starting to get it."

"I know but—"

He placed his index finger over her lips. "No *but*. You and Adam have been wonderful for Brian. You've made a huge difference in his life." Mike hesitated a moment, not sure if the next thought that popped in his head was something he should share, but his mouth didn't seem to care what his filters thought. "And mine."

The shock and regret in her big brown eyes immediately softened. A glint of moisture glistened at him, and, for a split second, he worried he'd said something to make her cry.

"Back at you," she whispered into his finger.

Oh, Lord. Was this it? Was that the cue that every single guy looked for? The one that usually came at the end of the date and said "kiss the girl"? Could he really be seeing raw hunger in her eyes? Did he dare? But she wasn't moving. Didn't pull back.

He inched his head a little closer, hoping she wouldn't retreat, and, slipping his finger out of the way, let his mouth land softly against hers. His heart galloped in his tightening chest. Any minute he expected her to back off in abject horror at his forwardness. Instead her arms snaked around his neck, and she burrowed even closer. Lord, she felt so good. So right. So … perfect. How horrible would it be if he stood here just a little longer? In public view. *Blast*.

Taking a half step back, he let his hands slide to her hips. "I, uh, … would give my right arm for a comfortable sofa and a little privacy."

"I was thinking the backseat of an old Chevy would work." Her forehead dropped against his shoulder. "Did I say that out loud?"

His chest rumbled with muffled laughter. "Yeah, you did. And you have no idea how sorry I am that I don't have a backseat." Sucking in a deep breath, he took two steps back. "I have to be home soon for Brian. We should probably finish the game."

Annette nodded, her cheeks slightly flushed. "Right. The game."

Those few words had come out slow and hesitant. He hoped she wasn't considering for even a second that he was blowing smoke. Reaching out and placing a finger under her chin, he lifted her face. "I really do wish this could last all night."

Annette barely nodded, his finger still tilting her head upward.

"Would you be willing to agree to a second date, or do I need to wait the appropriate few days and call?"

The sweet smile he'd grown rather fond of teased her lips into a perfect half-moon. "I think we can agree to another date."

"Free next Saturday night?"

She nodded. "Casual?"

"No." He grinned back at her. "I have something else in mind for our second date."

"So how was the date?"

From her spot on the gymnasium bleacher, Annette spun left to the direction of the voice.

"Oh, don't look so surprised." Emily took a seat beside her. "Maggie and Adam came by the shop yesterday when I was there. They wanted to see the new uniforms. Maggie may have mentioned something about being home with Adam and Bethany on Friday night, while you went out with Brian's dad."

"What are you doing here?"

"Nice dodge. I thought I'd come watch practice. Doug really is great with kids, don't ya think?"

"Mmm. He is." Annette was thrilled to shift attention away from her.

"So when's the next date?" Emily kept her eyes on the group of kids on the court.

"Who said there was a first date?"

Emily turned, dipping her chin, and glared at Annette with a look that most likely made her students cringe.

"Okay. I give. I had a great time."

"Good. Where'd you go?" Emily returned her attention to the practice below.

"Bowling."

Emily's head snapped around again. "Bowling?"

The memory had Annette grinning from ear to ear. She'd been doing that a lot lately. Maggie was the only one to call her on it. So far. "Yeah. We had a lot of fun."

Considering the response for a little bit, Emily finally nodded. "I bet you did. And now?"

"We're going out again Saturday." Every day their telephone conversations grew longer. And when Mike had to cut things off for work or Brian, Mike would call back later—often after Brian had gone to bed—and they'd talk even more. She still didn't understand how they hadn't run out of topics for conversation. The interesting thing for her was how she'd always thought, if she ever met someone new, she wouldn't be able to talk about Tom. That any mention of the first love of her life would somehow be a threat to another man. But not Mike. He understood what it was like to lose a mate. And rather than feel threatened, he asked about Tom. How they'd met. How long they'd dated. What the wedding was like. When the kids were born. He especially seemed fascinated by the early years, when they were building the business. It had been cathartic for her to share how she'd felt so alone and isolated in ICU while some crazed drug lord gunned for her husband's business and maybe even her children.

"More bowling?" Emily asked.

"I don't know what he has planned this time either."

"Ooh. A man with surprises." Emily's gaze remained riveted on her fiancé.

"Do you recognize the tall kid behind Doug?"

Eyes wide, Emily looked to the boy then back to Annette. "Do you really think having the bully on the team is a smart idea?"

"Mike and I were chatting, and we agreed. Learning true teamwork could be a good thing for him."

"I won't argue with you about the positive effects of sports on children, but the bully ..." Emily returned her gaze to the court. "How did you talk him into it?"

"Like Adam, he's not good enough for the school team but enjoys the sport. At first he made a fuss about playing with rejects. But I could tell he really did want to participate, so it wasn't a hard push for him to sign up. Eddie's father liked the idea too."

"His father's involved in this?"

Annette nodded. "Mike gave him a call. He didn't like the idea of the two boys on the same team if there wasn't full parental support behind it."

"Makes sense. What did the father say?"

"Both he and his wife had been looking for a way to get Eddie more involved in extracurricular activities, but Eddie hadn't shown any interest until this. They're almost as excited about it as we are."

"Huh." Emily shrugged. "Well, I'm no expert, but, from up here, things seem to be going pretty well."

"Yeah, I think so too," Annette said. "Doug came to school every afternoon for a few minutes to talk with the kids as a team. Prepare them for what's going to happen at practice. Show them around the gym. Get the special needs kids used to him, before he starts working with them. I'm so impressed with how he seems to instinctively know what each child needs. You've got a great guy there."

"I do." Emily's face brightened. "And so do you."

Annette really did. Every day whatever it was growing between her and Mike felt stronger and more important. She never would have thought she could care so much after only a few weeks. And yet she did care. A lot. Knowing that, in a little more than twenty-four hours, she would be on her second real date made her want to sing. Loudly. And she couldn't carry a tune. Tomorrow night was not coming fast enough.

CHAPTER TEN

Standing at the massive entryway of Annette's house, Mike sucked in a calming breath and rang the bell. He'd been as nervous about tonight as he'd been about last week. For their first date, concerned how Brian would do with the sitter for longer than three hours or so, Mike had intentionally kept their evening short. Tonight he hoped to enjoy the night without those constraints of time. His stomach did another flip, and a part of him wondered if he would ever get over this nervous anticipation every time he thought of being with Annette. And that was simply occupying the same room. He didn't dare let his mind wander to being with her in an intimate encounter. Remembering the kiss last week was enough to send his hormone levels soaring. He most definitely could not go there. Not yet.

"Hi." Annette opened the door, her face immediately softening when she noticed the gift. "You're going to spoil me."

"I saw it at the grocery store and couldn't resist." Holding out the small teddy bear in a basketball uniform, he wasn't going to mention he'd been to two toy stores and one gift shop before he stumbled onto the bear at the supermarket. "He needed a good home."

Annette scooped the stuffed animal against her chest, and Mike wished he could change places with the bear.

"I'll have to find a special place for him." She waved Mike into the house and gestured for him to take a seat in the living room. "I'll settle him in my room and be right back."

The mere mention of her bedroom had his libido on

high alert. He was really glad for the open patio doors, refreshing breezes, and the chance for a little distraction. The last thing he needed tonight was to come off as a randy teenager with a one-track mind. Even if his mind wasn't too far from just that.

"Okay. I'm all set. Where are we going?"

"I found a restaurant across town with a little piano bar, and tonight's musical highlights are the crooners." She'd mentioned in passing about discovering Tony Bennett's duet CDs after watching a PBS special with Lady Gaga singing on one of his recordings. Annette had bought that CD, fallen in love with the great remakes of the old favorites with popular singers, and bought all the others as well. He took a gamble that she'd like that era of music even without the pop stars.

"That sounds fabulous, but I'd better warn you I won't be able to resist singing along."

The momentary knot that had formed in his chest when she'd said the word *but* now loosened with the rest of her sentence, and a smile teased his lips. "We can sing together."

"Ha. You say that now. Wait till you discover I can't carry a tune to save my life."

She sauntered off to the car, and Mike's gaze shot straight to the gentle sway of her hips. He doubted seriously there was one imperfect bone—or note—in that woman's body.

Annette couldn't remember a more magical night. The tiny continental restaurant was heaven, the food spectacular, and the piano player had an array of tunes from Frank Sinatra to Michael Bublé. Every time the urge to sing along crept up, she shoved another forkful of food into her mouth.

"Sorry that took so long." Mike slid back into his seat. Liz was sitting again with Brian and Mike had taken a few moments to step outside and call. He and Annette had stopped for before-dinner cocktails on the beach and had already passed the three-hour time frame he'd been gone from Brian last week.

"Is something wrong? Should we head home?"

"No, no. Everything is fine." He took a sip of his drink, set down the glass, and smiled at her. "I can tell from the way your foot keeps tapping that you're enjoying the music."

"Totally."

"Who's your favorite?"

"Well, of the songs he's played so far, I'd have to say, 'They Can't Take That Away from Me,' but 'I Get a Kick out of You' is a close second. What about you?"

"Wrong era. I'm more of a U2 sort of guy."

"In that case it was especially nice of you to bring me here."

"I had ulterior motives."

"Such as?" She loved it when his eyes sparkled with mischief.

Mike pushed back his seat and, standing, extended his hand across the small table. "Dance with me?"

The quaint restaurant sported a small patch of wooden floor beside the piano. An older couple, who moved as though they'd been dancing together their entire lives, glided along the floor to a peppier rendition of "The Shadow of Your Smile." By the time Annette and Mike reached the small space, the pianist began to sing Frank's popular hit "All the Way."

With every note played, she curled closer into his arms, feeling lost and safe at the same time. As the soothing male voice crooned throughout the room, "if you let me love you," Mike's hold on her tightened. They swayed across the floor in a single fluid movement as though they too had been dancing together for all their lives. She wanted to stay like this, dancing in his arms.

Every word of the song seemed to be directed straight at her, addressing any doubts or fears that might have been tickling the back of her mind, as each day passed and she found herself more and more entranced with Michael

Becker. But here and now, she was sure of at least one thing. Wherever this new road led them, there was no turning back. She was in deep with both feet, for as far and long as he'd have her.

Gladly Mike would have danced with Annette in his arms all night. All year. Every word sung seemed to be directed straight at him, addressing the few doubts and fears that might have been kicking at the back of his mind as he found himself more and more entranced with Annette Deluca. Whether she knew it or not, he was completely hers. Now all he had to do was bide his time and hopefully worm his way into her heart as deeply as she'd made herself at home in his.

The pianist played another tune before taking his break. Mike considered for a brief moment if the few patrons would notice if he and Annette kept dancing to their own music. He wondered if it was as hard for her to pull apart as it had been for him. "They have a wonderful dessert menu," he said easing farther away. Willing his hands to let go of her.

Annette seemed to struggle to find her smile. "I don't think I could eat another bite."

Without dessert there was no excuse to stay. To wait for another set. To hold her in his arms again. To feel her warmth nestled against him.

"But I wouldn't mind a cup of tea," she added.

Hallelujah. He wasn't ready to end this date yet. Holding out her seat for her, he took advantage and let his fingers brush slightly against her back, before returning to his own seat. Unwilling to leave the table again, he quickly shot off a text to the sitter to check on Brian: *HOW'S IT GOING?* The response was immediate: *FINE. STOP CHECKING ON US AND ENJOY YOUR DATE.*

"Something funny?" Annette asked.

"I've been scolded by Liz and told to stop checking up

on them." Determined to do as advised, he slipped the phone into his pocket.

"Seems like sound advice." She continued to smile up at him, as he ordered two cups of tea, but he could see a whirlpool of emotions hiding behind those soft chestnut-colored eyes. And that worried him.

An awkward silence fell over the table, and Mike wondered if he'd gone too far. If maybe she'd not been ready for this much attention from him. With every passing day he felt as though he'd known Annette for years. When Karen passed, he never really believed there'd be another woman in his life who made him feel so much at home. But everything was comfortable with Annette. Not even mentioning Karen's name was a problem. After all, no woman wants to play second fiddle to a dead wife, but Annette wasn't like that.

With her, they could talk about their late spouses with love and affection, and understand that, like multiple children, it in no way diminished how much love Mike had for Annette. And, yes. He loved her. The real kind Sinatra and the piano player crooned about. The kind that went together like a horse and carriage. And wasn't that a problem? There was so much more to consider than just how he felt about her.

The waiter reappeared with two small teapots of water and their choice of teas. Annette thanked the server and quickly began dipping the tea bag in her cup of water. Just as Mike was about to ask any inane question to break the tension, she laid her wrists on the edge of the table and lifted her chin high. "What are we doing?"

He had to think a minute. Too unsure of what she meant, he had no choice. "Excuse me?"

"I know I should keep my mouth shut, play the game, see where this goes. If it goes anywhere at all. But I can't do that. It's not my style."

"No." He smiled. "I don't imagine waiting for anything is your style."

Shaking her head, she returned his easy grin, though hers was considerably more unsteady. "Why are you doing all this?" She waved from the table to the pianist. "What do you want from me? Because, quite frankly, I don't remember a roll in the hay requiring this much attention."

Her words stunned him momentarily. "You're right. As much as I would love to have my hands all over you, this is not about sex. All I'd need to find *a roll in the hay*, as you put it, is a short while at a local bar and a little free-flowing booze. I'm not after that. Never have been."

He'd hoped she would say something. All she did was continue to stare at him with laserlike precision that had him wondering if she could read his mind, but, if not, she was most certainly determining the veracity of his words. Honesty was the best policy. "I don't want to say the wrong thing."

That clearly caught her by surprise. She eased forward slightly. "I don't understand."

Brushing aside the teacup, he stretched his hand out to fold it over hers. "I'm a one-woman man. For years I thought that woman was Karen. Thought it would always be Karen. Thought I'd never find anyone else who … fit. Until you."

Her eyes widened, and he could feel the tremble of her fingers beneath his.

In for a penny, in for a pound. "I don't think I could handle losing you too."

She closed her eyes, and his already hammering heart stuttered to a halt. When she lifted her lids, he saw a clarity that had been missing since they'd sat down again. "I don't want to lose you either. So what do we do about it?"

Annette was sure, if life got any better, her face would split in two from smiling so much. Just a few short weeks ago she almost dreaded another holiday without Tom, and now she could hardly wait for Christmas. And every holiday after that. Not that every holiday was guaranteed. Over tea she and Mike had agreed to take things one day at a time.

They weren't kids anymore, and both clearly recognized when something was just right. But, in light of Brian's challenges, they'd agreed *slow* was the only way to proceed. Especially if they wanted this budding relationship to last, and she wanted that very much.

Mike pulled into the drive. She could tell from the way his eyes darted from the dashboard clock to her front door that he was itching to check up on his son again.

"Do you want to call about Brian and then come in for some dessert? Or maybe it would be best if you got back to him."

"No." Mike's eyes twinkled with a hint of humor. "I've got to learn not to be so overprotective. If Liz needs me, she'll call. I would love to come in, if it's not too late."

"Not at all. I think there's cheesecake in the fridge. Assuming the kids didn't eat it all in one sitting." Shoving open the front door, Annette listened for the sound of her family. A selfish little part of her had hoped they'd be in bed, and she could be alone with Mike. "Follow me. I think I hear the TV in the other room."

Off the kitchen, the kids sat in the family room, sprawled on the sofa, watching some movie with a loud car-chase scene. Most likely Adam's choice. Maggie was installed in the recliner across the way, working on a crossword puzzle—though Annette had no idea how Maggie could think straight with the surround sound on.

"Mom." Bethany looked up and waved.

For a split second, Annette thought she saw disappointment cross her face, but now her daughter was all smiles. Adam was another story. The boy looked from Annette to Mike, Adam's icy gaze enough to chill the room.

"Hi, honey." She moved farther into the room, expecting the usual hug and kiss, only to have Adam push to his feet and leave without a word. "What the heck?"

"Maybe I shouldn't have come in after all." Mike stared down the hall after Adam.

"Nonsense." But she didn't get it. There hadn't been a single sign of discomfort or disapproval from either of her children. And now they'd spent all night worrying about how their date would affect Brian, but the one to pitch a silent fit was her son.

"I'm afraid that might be my fault." Maggie set aside her paper and stood. "I was talking with the kids earlier. I said something about how nice it was that you'd found someone who made you as happy as their dad did, and Adam didn't react well."

"I see." Annette's gaze turned to the empty hall.

"You can't really blame him," Bethany said from her space on the sofa.

Maggie sighed. "Mike, can I get you something to drink? We've got everything, including scotch and bourbon."

"Actually"—Annette turned to her house manager and friend—"I promised him cheesecake."

"Good choice." Maggie spun about toward the kitchen. "Cheesecake coming up."

Mike glanced at Annette, and she clearly read the question in his eyes. "I'm sure. Why don't you help Maggie cut five slices? We'll all join you in a minute."

Bless the man, he didn't argue or make a fuss, just offered her a reassuring smile and fell in line behind Maggie.

"Want to tell me what's going on?" Annette sat beside her daughter.

"Nothing really. But you can't blame Adam for being upset."

"I'll talk to Adam about Adam. I want to know what's going on with you."

Bethany grabbed at a nearby cushion, then, sighing, tossed it aside again. "I know in my head that Dad wouldn't want you to be alone the rest of your life. I get it. I'm not stupid."

"And you're not a little girl anymore either."

That made Bethany smile. "Thanks. Like I said, I know this is in my head, but it's just going to take the rest of me a while to catch up. Mike's a nice guy. It's just … a little hard sometimes."

Annette pulled her daughter into a tight embrace. "It's

hard on me too."

"Really?" Bethany mumbled in her ear.

"Really." Annette didn't pull away, until her daughter released her hold. "We're going to talk about this some more. Later. Right now I need to talk to Adam, and there's a slice of cheesecake in the kitchen with everyone's name on it."

Bethany smiled just enough to let Annette know her daughter really would be okay with all of this. "I love you, Mom."

"Love you too, baby." Annette patted her daughter's arm, and the two walked off in opposite directions. Reaching her son's room, Annette tapped lightly on the door frame. At least he hadn't closed the door. That was a good sign. "May I come in?"

Adam sat in front of his Gamebox and nodded.

"Want to tell me what's on your mind?" She eased onto the bed beside him.

Putting down the controller, he gave her a halfhearted shrug.

"Is this because of something Maggie said?"

"I guess." Without actually picking up the controller again, Adam continued to fidget with it, before looking his mother in the face. "Mike's a nice guy and all, but he's not Dad."

"No." Annette sucked in a breath. "He's not."

"I mean"—Adam looked away again—"I like him, and it was okay going to Wednesday-night pizza and stuff with him and Brian, but—"

"But that's different than just him and me going out?"

"Maggie says Dad wouldn't want you to be alone forever. Do you think that's true?"

"I'd like to think so. I know if I'd been the one who died, I wouldn't want Daddy to be sad without me."

"But I miss him." Adam leaned into her, wrapping his arms around her waist. Now that he was growing up, hugging Mom and snuggling with Mom was considered only for little kids. The gesture had her heart swelling and her eyes watering.

"I miss him too. I'll always miss him. But the heart is an interesting muscle. There's no limit to how much love it holds. I only have you and Bethany, but, when you guys grow up and have children of your own, I'm going to love them as much as I love you. And, if I live long enough to meet my great grandchildren, I'll love them too. I won't love you any less because I have more people to love."

He eased back and looked up at her. "Then you still love Dad?"

"Always will." It was all she could do to blink back the tears.

"And Brian's dad really makes you as happy as Dad did?"

This time all Annette could do was nod. She'd only had a few weeks with Mike, but she hadn't been as happy as she was now since losing Tom.

"Then I guess I'll catch up too."

"Catch up?"

"That's what Bethany called it. But we're not going to have to watch you two kissing and doing other mushy stuff, are we?"

That had her laughing. "Let's agree that, for now, there will be no public mushiness."

Adam's head bobbed. "Okay."

"You up for some cheesecake?"

His eyes lit up. "Maggie wouldn't let us have any until you got home."

"I take it that's a yes."

Adam didn't answer; he gave her a sly grin and ran out of the room, his growing feet slapping heavily against the wood floors. If only everything in life could be solved with a slice of cheesecake.

CHAPTER ELEVEN

"**G**o, Adam!" Hands cupping his mouth, Mike hollered loud and clear. "Cut to the hoop."

Annette was on her feet, beside him, hooting. She didn't have a clue what to shout out that might help. All she knew was Adam had the ball at the other end of the court, and that was a good thing for scoring opportunity. All the rest of the rules about lines, boundaries, and dribbling were completely lost on her.

Almost at the same time as Mike had yelled, Doug had given Adam the same instructions. Her son did as the two men had directed: drew the defense toward him and passed the ball to Jamie, a team member with Down syndrome. Jamie, taking his time—not something often seen in a regular game—aimed and flung the ball up and into the basket. The crowd erupted, and Annette clapped until her palms hurt.

"This really is exciting." Sitting on the other side of Annette, Maile Everrett leaned in closer. "I'd forgotten how much fun it was going to Billy's school games."

Though it astounded Mike when, one by one, the Everrett clan turned up in the bleachers, Annette wasn't even slightly surprised by the show of support. Emily had explained, with the high school program, few people had showed up at the first couple of games to cheer on the kids—only the parents and perhaps a few friends. As those players got better, more attendees came, packing the stands. Not wanting any of the kids in tonight's game to feel slighted, Emily made it a point to mention the game to her mother, brother, and friends.

This close-knit family had taught Annette the true

meaning of solidarity. The only people missing were Nick and Kara, since little Catherine had come down with a slight post-vaccinations fever. Jim was on another mission, so his wife, Lexie, was in town for a few days and here cheering on Adam and Brian and even Eddie. Billy and Angela were on Maile's other side. They'd brought their baby girl, Isabella, as well as Nick's son, Bradley. Emily and Bethany were on the lower bleachers, closer to the action. Although Emily cheered for the boys, she did a lot of smiling and thumbs-up pointing at Doug for his coaching efforts. Bethany followed more closely in her mother's footsteps, just hooting and hollering for both her brother and Brian.

One of the away-team members passed the ball, and, instead of reaching the desired teammate, Brian, guarding the player, tapped the ball out of play. Once again Mike sprang to his feet, shouting, "Attaboy, Brian." Though it wasn't necessarily the right thing to have done, having Brian do anything was a major breakthrough.

Unlike Adam, who occasionally glanced at the crowd when his name was called, Brian focused on the ball, watching and moving in tandem with his assigned player. Annette's heart swelled with pride. She'd come to understand just how hard doing those two simple tasks simultaneously were for Brian. Because of his friendship with Adam, and Doug taking his time to familiarize the special ed kids with himself and the gym, Brian had been more cooperative about his participation. Not so much for some of the other children. Annette had heard that one of the boys on the other team hid every day after school to avoid practice, until one of the teachers finally had to escort him there.

The fear of change was overwhelming for some of these kids. Or perhaps the fear of participation. She still wasn't sure, but she was delighted to see all the children on the court looking pleased, if a bit like preschoolers playing "herd" ball. So she understood expecting Brian to respond to the crowd was too much, but she and Mike cheered him on anyway. She truly believed, though Brian didn't acknowledge them, deep down he knew they were cheering for him.

With only a few minutes left in the game, the other team had come within two points of catching up and just a moment ago had tied the score. For as raw as Annette's nerves were, she'd have thought the children were playing in the Olympics. Watching the clock tick by slowly, she almost didn't see Eddie dribbling up the court to shoot and score. Another wave of cheers and whistles surrounded her.

"Nice shot, Eddie," Annette shouted seconds before the final horn blew. The boy's team had won the game by only two points.

"Wow," Billy's wife, Angela, said, shaking her head. "That was a nail-biter."

"Tell me about it." Annette leaned closer to Mike, knowing, if she sidled next to him, he'd shoot out his hand for her to hold. She loved all the small silent understandings they'd come to. Some days she swore he could actually read her mind.

From where she stood, she could easily see the children below. The teams crossed the court to shake the opposing team members' hands and then, she noticed, on their way out of the gym, Adam and Eddie doing a high five, followed by Eddie giving Brian a high five too. She knew it was mostly because Brian felt the need to copy everything Adam did, but she liked the idea that Eddie was, indeed, learning more about teamwork. This was especially true since, as Adam had reported to her, even though she'd cut back to only joining the boys for lunch one day a week, Eddie no longer terrorized the geeks and misfits.

"Okay. Down to the locker rooms to wait for the boys." Mike climbed over the row in front of him. Still holding on to Annette, he waited for her to land beside him before extending his other hand to the Everrett matriarch.

"Don't you even think about it." Maile slapped at his hand. "I'm not that old yet."

Annette laughed. "He helped me. I certainly hope I'm not that old yet."

"At your age it doesn't matter." Maile chuckled beside her, waving off the comment. "At my age, climbing down myself is a statement."

"Ah. Got it."

Holding back a grin, Mike squeezed Annette's fingers a little tighter. Maile was definitely a force to be reckoned with. "This may sound a bit silly, but I feel like a real parent."

Annette's face scrunched in confusion.

Holding her hand, Mike and she continued to work their way toward to the gym floor. "Today I drove my son to another school to play in a ball game. For the last thirty-plus minutes, I sat in the bleachers, cheering for my child, like all the other parents here. It felt so normal."

There were no words for the emotions gurgling inside her. Sharing this moment with Mike had her nearly tearing up. So many things the average parent took for granted. So much she still didn't understand but was slowly learning.

"Are we all heading out for a celebratory ice cream?" Billy asked, one arm around his wife, the other held the infant carrier with Isabella.

"No." Mike shook his head. "I don't think that's a good idea tonight. We're going to go home to familiar territory and lay low."

"Understood." Billy gave a curt dip of his chin, and Annette got the feeling Billy understood things better than any of them.

"Besides," Annette said, "we promised the boys we'd do the Christmas tree at Brian's tonight."

Billy frowned and looked over his shoulder to Annette. "Christmas is only a few days away. Isn't it a little late to be putting up a tree?"

"We don't usually do trees at all," Mike answered, continuing their descent. "But we've been to Annette and Adam's several times since they've had the tree up. Brian keeps staring at the lights. When he was young, the tree just sent him into a tizzy. Now he wants one of his own, so tonight's the night. I figure they'll be on an adrenaline high from a well-played game—at least Adam will. Brian's harder to predict lately. So we might as well accomplish something while waiting for him to wind down."

At the head of the line, Billy reached the end of the

bleachers first and directed his wife down the gymnasium main hall.

"So," Maile reached the next to last bleacher, "will you and Brian be joining us for Christmas Eve dinner with Annette and the children?"

Annette noticed Mike's shoulders sag before he answered. "Thank you for the invitation but new places are difficult on Brian. Especially new places with lots of people and the commotion involved in presents and gift-giving. It's best if we treat the day as close to any other day as possible."

That same furrow that appeared earlier on Billy's face formed now on his mother's brow. "I suppose you're right. But if anything changes, you're always welcome."

"Thank you."

This time it was Annette who squeezed Mike's hand, offering a little emotional reassurance. They'd discussed how to handle Christmas multiple times. Some days, when Brian had had an exceptionally eventless day, Mike had thought *maybe*. Then, on others, when Brian seemed to be on everyone's last nerve, Mike knew a big commotion like that wouldn't work. Tonight was a test of sorts. How well would Brian do with Annette and both her children at his home in a holidaylike event? Would Brian's familiarity and comfort with his own surroundings be enough to maintain his calm with the addition of new people *and* a Christmas tree? She prayed it would. If tonight went well, the new plans for Christmas involved the Beckers and the Delucas celebrating the holidays as one family.

She loved that idea. One family. Integrating the two worlds would make *The Brady Bunch* seem like a walk in the park. Even though Adam and Bethany appeared to be on board with the growing relationship, and Brian had begun to accept the Deluca family's involvement in almost everything as part of his routine, she and Mike were still taking their time.

If what they had was real, and she knew it was, then she had nothing to lose taking things one day at a time. But both she and Mike had a goal.

"You doing okay?" Mike asked softly over his shoulder.

"I'm doing more than okay."

"Good." As the final couple to reach ground level, Mike lifted Annette over the last row of bleachers, slowly releasing his hold on her.

Before she knew what hit her, Mike had tugged her from the moving crowd and into a nearby hallway cutout. Her back to the corner, his arms protectively against the wall on either side of her, his lips fell on hers. The kiss was hot and fast and all-consuming. Just as suddenly as he'd tugged her into the corner, he pulled away. "One day," he mumbled against her forehead.

"I know," she said. "One day. One family."

CHAPTER TWELVE

"What a fabulous day for a wedding." Annette Deluca hurried into the ready suite at the beachfront hotel and hung her bridesmaid dress on the nearest door. "Sorry I'm a little late. Why is it, the minute you're ready to leave home, everyone suddenly needs Mom? You'd think no one else on the island had any idea how to find missing shoes, referee sibling squabbles, or make a peanut butter and jelly sandwich."

From her seat at the nearby vanity, bride-to-be Emily Everrett looked over her shoulder. "Peanut butter and jelly?"

"Four o'clock is Brian's snack time." Annette huffed at the roomful of women layered in various stages of formal attire. "It's not that I mind making sandwiches, but Adam is—"

"Old enough to make his own sandwich," Maggie Maplewood provided, sliding in the suite door behind her boss and friend. "And one for Brian too."

"Exactly," Annette agreed, sinking into the overstuffed sofa. "Just give me a few seconds to catch my breath and cool off, before I have to slip into that sheath."

Maggie lifted a polite brow at her employer.

"I mean"—Annette grinned—"that beautiful dress that I've spent three weeks dieting for."

"Good save," Ava Everrett, one of the bride's sisters, said. "I'm just thankful we're not in lavender taffeta. I look horrible in lavender, and I'm not going to discuss taffeta."

"I don't mind taffeta near as much as tulle." Kathleen Everrett slipped a hairpin in place. "This summer my college roommate"–she turned to face her sister Ava—"You remember Jami?"

Both Ava and Emily nodded.

"Well, we looked like peach broomsticks. Strapless satin with a ruched bodice and, Lord help me, layers and layers of orange tulle sprouting out from below the knee, like a lampshade on a drunk."

Annette couldn't help herself. "You've seen that many drunken lampshades?"

Shaking her head, Kathleen stuck another pin in her hair. "I've seen enough drunks wearing lampshades to know what I'm talking about."

"Must be the San Francisco lifestyle," Ava chimed in.

"Well everyone can rest assured, there will be no tulle, peach, or any other obnoxious color in my bridal party," one of the other bridesmaids said pointedly.

"On behalf of all the bridesmaids in the world"— Kathleen waved her arms in a grand gesture and bowed her head in reverence—"I thank you."

"You guys are something else." Annette pushed to her feet. "I guess it's time to squeeze into this dress."

"I don't understand what you're talking about." Ava raised Kathleen's zipper. "I hope to God that I look as good as you when I have two teenagers."

Hands on her waist, Kathleen looked over her shoulder at her older sister. "Something you want to share, sis?"

"Nope." Ava smiled at her audience. "Let me get through at least one anniversary before you have me in the maternity ward."

"Just remember, you're not getting any younger." Emily batted her freshly mascara-laden lashes over a cheesy grin.

"Sisters." Kathleen and Ava echoed.

Annette laughed out loud. Again. She was so happy to be a part of this day. No one was more surprised than her to be included in the bridal shenanigans. When Emily had first mentioned having Annette in the wedding party, she didn't take her friend seriously. After all, she was quite a bit older than Emily and hadn't lived on the island that long. Still, on a day like today, there were no years standing between any of these women. Everyone was having a great time.

"You're next." Waving a finger at Annette, Maile Everrett, the family matriarch, rose from her seat by the makeup artist.

"Oh, Mom," one of her daughters said on a long breath. "You look fabulous."

"You were expecting maybe I would look like an old fish wife?" Maile came around the chair, her full figure swaddled in a formfitting floor-length gown of dark purple.

So used to seeing her in bright floral housedresses, Annette was as stunned as the girls to see Maile's Mae West figure. "I'm with your daughters. Wow."

"Thank you." Maile's eyes twinkled, and Annette was pretty sure, under the layers of makeup, the Everrett family matriarch was blushing.

Thirty minutes later, her makeup done and her dress on, Annette sucked in a deep breath for Ava to raise her zipper. Taking a step back, Ava let out a loud whistle. "Talk about hiding your light under a bushel. Mike is going to swallow his tongue when he sees you."

Annette spun about to get a glimpse of herself in the full-length mirror. Ava was right. The dress was very flattering. Emily had done a great job of picking gowns suited to each woman's frame. Annette hadn't felt this beautiful in a very long time. A giddy energy gurgled inside her at the thought of walking down the aisle and Mike watching her come toward him. Her mind flashed back to that day years ago when Tom had waited for her at the front of a church. She never thought another man could make her heart sputter again, but here she was like a teen on prom night.

"Okay, ladies." The drill sergeant of a wedding coordinator clapped her hands. "Time to leave for the church. No bride of mine has ever been late."

Like raw recruits, one by one the entourage followed the coordinator out the door and down the hall to the waiting limousine. Annette couldn't have been more excited or nervous if today had been her own wedding day. Now wouldn't that be something?

For the hundredth time since the groomsmen had claimed their places at the front of the church, Mike resisted the urge to tug at his collar. He hadn't been this nervous at his own wedding. Of course it wasn't Doug and Emily's nuptials that had him as anxious as a cat in a roomful of rockers; it was the ring for Annette in his breast pocket that had his palms sweating.

Well, not the ring itself. Not even the question that came with the ring. Ever since that night of bowling, he'd known that he and Annette were meant to be together. The ease of Christmas Eve followed by a low-key but delightful Christmas day had cemented the idea of *together forever* in his mind.

Despite the expected challenges of the overly stimulating holiday upsetting Brian and his routine, Mike could not have hoped for things to go more smoothly. Annette's children had taken the pared-down celebration in stride. Adam had been the perfect buffer for any surprises. Even Bethany had taken on a protective attitude toward Brian. More than once Mike had actually forgotten they had not always been one family. First thing Saturday morning he'd gone to the jeweler to look around and had come home with what he hoped was the perfect ring.

Earlier today, when Doug found out that Mike had been carrying the velvet box around for almost a week, waiting for the perfect time, Doug had insisted today was the day. Mike had to agree that few places would be more romantic than New Year's Day on the beach, under the stars, with a favorite love song playing in the background—though Mike didn't see eye to eye with Doug about a bunch of happy, and possibly tipsy, wedding guests to cheer him on. Despite Mike's arguments that today was Emily's day, Doug convinced him that proposing to Annette would be the best wedding gift for him and Emily. Now Mike wished things would hurry up and move along, so he could get Annette alone on the beach.

Each of the bridesmaids eased their way up the long aisle. They were a lovely sight, but it was Annette who stole his breath. He'd thought her beautiful from the first time he'd seen her standing at his front door, but tonight she surpassed the beauty of every sappy poem ever written. Even Emily, as stunning a bride as she was, didn't hold a candle to Annette.

The music drew to a close as Billy handed off his sister to his best friend. Mike had to admit Doug and Emily made a mighty fine couple. The way their loving gazes clung to each other, Mike felt certain a golden wedding anniversary was definitely painted in their future. By the time the priest pronounced the couple husband and wife, Mike had patted his breast pocket at least a dozen times. Every time his eyes met with Annette's, his heart beat a little faster.

When the newly married couple turned to face the crowd, the guests burst into heavy applause. Mike was only a few minutes away from his turn to walk down the aisle arm in arm with Annette. A high school freshman on his first date couldn't have been more excited about the prospect of having a girl at his side.

"They look so happy," Annette whispered out of the side of her mouth.

"That's because they are," he whispered back, extending his elbow to her.

Annette's smile stretched across her face. "That they are."

Sucking in a deep calming breath, Mike fell in step with the woman who he hoped in the not-too-distant future would be *his* bride.

The old Isley Brothers' tune "Shout" blared through the hall, out to the veranda, and across the beach for all to kick their heels up. Annette couldn't remember when she'd last danced so much or had so much fun. She and Mike had done everything from the twist to the most absurd rendition of the tango that had kept half the guests doubling over in laughter. But this old tune—that had to be the national wedding reception anthem—had every person, young or ancient, on the dance floor bopping up and down. Annette had stooped about as low as she could go as the music got a "little bit softer" for the last time. When the volume grew louder again, she nearly toppled over as everyone sprang up, arms and legs flailing. Before she even realized she was off balance, Mike had reached out to steady her. Something he had been doing quite often over the last few weeks, and she was growing pretty darn used to it.

"Think maybe we should sit this one out?" Mike asked.

"Oh, yeah. Right after I drink a gallon of water."

"If all the single women would please come center stage," the DJ announced.

"Sound like it's time for the bride to toss the bouquet." Annette flopped rather unceremoniously in the nearest chair.

Mike took the seat beside her. "Aren't you going up there? You are single."

"I am." *Sort of.* "But I have no intention of grappling with a dozen or more twentysomethings bound and determined to take that bunch of flowers home tonight."

"Oh, you could take them with one hand tied behind your back."

Why was it so easy for this man to make her laugh? "Not tonight I can't. The brothers Isley have worn me out."

Mike's eyes sparkled with amusement. "Let me get you that water."

As predicted, about a dozen women of all shapes, sizes, and, to Annette's surprise, ages, lined up several feet behind the bride. Her back to the crowd, Emily raised and lowered her arm once, twice, and then, on the third lift, flung the flowers overhead, across the room, and right into her mother's lap. Poor Maile looked so stunned, even the bouquet-catching brigade had to chuckle. It took the woman all of ten seconds to gather her bearings and toss the bouquet back to the huddle of single women. A tall brunette, who Annette recognized as a teacher from the high school, caught the soaring blooms and seemed perfectly content to ignore the unexpected detour they'd taken.

At Annette's side in time to watch Doug's silly antics—tugging down Emily's garter with his teeth, and with what looked to be half the US Navy cheering him on—Mike handed her a large glass of ice water. "Here you go."

"Thanks."

A small scuffle ensued when Doug tossed the garter into a healthy crowd of single men. Next the bride and the tall brunette clutching the bouquet to her chest changed places.

Annette took a long swallow of the refreshing water, set it aside, and smiled when Mike slipped his fingers around hers. With so little private time available, she'd come to cherish the small gestures of affection they could share in public. Holding hands like this was one of her favorites.

A Hercules clone in dress whites kneeled in front of the blushing schoolteacher and winked. Annette had a hard time believing that the family men she'd come to know and respect had at one time been swaggering sailors much like—no, probably exactly like—the confident and playful man in uniform on bended knee. Choosing to use his teeth, much the way Doug had, this handsome sailor had the stretchy band up the woman's leg and over her knee in no time. The crowd roared with laughter and applause, and the DJ switched the music to a much slower melody.

"Dance?" Mike pushed to his feet and held out his hand.

"I'd love to, but, if the speed picks up again, I'll be wanting the nearest chair."

"Agreed."

By now folding into his embrace, as they swayed softly across the floor, had become almost second nature. She fit just right against his chest. At least she thought so. They moved around the floor and out the doors. The music could still be heard on the terrace, but outdoor speakers helped. One song slipped into another, when she recognized "Thinking Out Loud" playing. When Ed Sheeran got to the part about "loving you 'til we're seventy," she curled closer into Mike's arms. The thought of staying right where she was until they were well into their seventies made her smile. And want.

"Annette." Mike cleared his throat.

"Yes?" As much as she hated losing any contact, she shifted enough to look up at him.

"I, I know we haven't been together very long by many people's standards, but I don't need more time to know how I feel. What I want."

A sudden surge of hope and panic stilled her heart.

"I love you more every day, Annette Deluca. I want to grow old with you. Help me start this year right. Marry me?"

Hope soared. Her heart lurched back to a steadier rhythm. She had to swallow hard to make her mouth move. "Yes." She smiled up at him. "Yes. Yes. And yes."

Their mouths came together in a press of lips and heart and soul. In the background the song continued on, crooning about "under thousands of stars," and a distant voice, warmed with laughter, mumbled, "I think she said yes."

EPILOGUE

Hand in hand, the new Mr. and Mrs. Michael Becker practically skipped down the church aisle.

In the foyer, dressed in an ankle length cream shift, her new husband at her side, and flanked by three good looking kids, Annette Deluca, now Becker, beamed. As a matter of fact, if the new bride and groom smiled any brighter, they wouldn't need power the rest of the evening.

"Brian is holding up really well," Nick Harper leaned into his friend. "They visited the church often and did multiple dry runs to prepare him. None of us were really sure, until now, if it would work. Amazing how resilient the human spirit is. That entire family has come so far since Christmas."

Luke "Brooklyn" Chapman had to agree with his former Navy buddy. Even Mr. Magoo could have seen the love bouncing between the bride and groom and their new blended family. Brooklyn was especially moved by Annette's son Adam, the protective barrier between his new brother Brian and the surrounding crowds.

Last in the receiving line, Brooklyn and his wife Sharla were next after Nick and Kara when Annette spotted him, squinting momentarily before connecting the dots. Bolting forward and out of line, she pulled him into a bone crushing hug, lingering longer than a simple hello. "I can't believe you came."

Momentarily, caught of guard, Brooklyn wrapped his arms around her and swallowed the lump in his throat.

"Uh hm," her new husband cleared his throat, the twinkle in his eyes softening his words, "Would you two like to be alone?"

Annette spun on her heal and patting Mike's arm, beamed up at him. "Sorry, I don't think we've had the time for formal introductions. Brooklyn. Mike."

Brooklyn stuck his hand out. "Congratulations. Wouldn't have missed this for the world."

Ever since he and his wife had come to Kona for the last team wedding, they'd been talking about returning for another visit. When he'd received the invitation from Annette, he and Sharla agreed this wedding couldn't be missed.

Not that they'd been close, he hadn't even seen Annette in person until she walked down the aisle little more than an hour ago. But, in his line of work, no matter how hard he and his men tried, some cases settled deep in a man's bones. Annette and her kids had been one of those. Even though he trusted Nick and Billy's word as much as his own, he still needed to make sure for himself that the right man had won Annette's heart.

"*The* Brooklyn?" One arm now looped around his wife's waist, Mike pumped Brooklyn's arm a little harder with the other. "So glad you made it. Thank you."

Both men knew the gratitude had little to do with attending the ceremony, but with Brooklyn's small part in keeping Annette and her kids safe from the men who had killed her late husband.

"My pleasure." And it was. He and his men had been charged with keeping Annette safe in LA from harm while Billy and his former team looked out for the kids here in Kona. It was Mike's job now to keep her happy, and in the little Brooklyn had seen so far, he had no doubts the man was up to the task.

"If you'll excuse me," the wedding coordinator interrupted. "The photographer needs you outside if we're going to stay on schedule."

Mike rolled his eyes, Annette let out a little sigh before turning back to Brooklyn. "We'll catch up later. Okay?"

He nodded and smiled at the two people following the general of a wedding planner with the same bubbly giddiness as a couple of barely legal kids. "It really is nice to see," he whispered to his wife, leaned over and kissed the tip of her nose. "Reminds me of us."

"Us?" she raised a brow at him.

"I mean, I know they're a bit older than we are and come with a ready made family, but no matter how raw a deal life hands you, fate can still bring that special someone to change everything."

Sharla stepped up on her tippy-toes and gently kissed his lips. "That it can. That it most definitely can."

EXCERPT FROM

SHELL GAME

Somewhere near the Afghan border

Whiskey Tango Foxtrot—WTF. From his rooftop perch Luke "Brooklyn" Chapman had a clear shot at the last barrier between his team and the American journalist they'd been assigned to bring home. Only two things stood in his way. Enough C4 to blow not only the entire compound but also every member of his SEAL team and Nick Harper's Explosive Ordnance Disposal team to kingdom come—and the woman wearing the frigging explosives.

Do not pass Go. Do not collect two hundred dollars. Blast...

Intel had screwed with them again. Brooklyn had gotten wind on his own of possible mines and other booby traps along the target compound that official channels had discarded as unreliable. That was why Brooklyn was once again working with EOD. He'd requested Nick's team for this mission, and, royally ticked off with the increased stream of failed missions, his CO had approved it. Nick and his team were good. Very good. The best. And Brooklyn trusted them as much as his own men. Which was something rare for a frogger to admit.

"Team Bravo reporting, target spotted. We have confirmation on explosives. C4. Over."

"Can you take him out? Over."

"Her," Brooklyn corrected.

Nick mumbled an obscenity on the other side.

Tell me about it. Protecting women and children was etched in bold caps on the unwritten list of what military men were fighting for—right above Mom's apple pie and just under the American Way. Over time Brooklyn had grown used to dealing with hostiles of varied ages and sizes—but he'd never get used to fighting women. And the key question at hand was whether or not this particular female was in harm's way of her own free will or by order of some male family member.

Too often there was not enough time to determine if the explosive-wearing fashionistas were the former or the latter. In this case, Brent Callahan, one of the EOD team, was on the surveillance systems. Thanks to his Persian heritage on his mother's side and having spent over a year at the Defense Language Institute, Brent could eavesdrop in five languages spoken within a one-mile radius. If the female in question would only say something in the next few seconds allotted to determine friendly or enemy, Brooklyn's last kill for Uncle Sam's Navy might not have to be a woman.

Across the way on Team Alpha, Billy "King Kona" Everrett and Doug Hamilton, rappelled down the south wall. Kenny Yates and Nick, Team Charlie, were nowhere to be seen. Which meant the hostiles couldn't see them either. The difference being Brooklyn knew his buddies were positioned to have Team Alpha's six.

Brother, how he wished Brent would speak up. In about fifteen seconds Billy would be in place, and Brooklyn would have to take the woman out. Ten.... Five.

"Hold your fire," Brent said in Brooklyn's earpiece. "Make that two hostages."

Whoever the woman was, Brent must have heard enough to know wearing this season's dynamite trend was not her idea. Brooklyn spoke into his mic. "Affirmative."

"Copy," Nick replied, followed by Billy's echo of the confirmation.

This unlucky woman would live to see another day. All the team had to do was diffuse the jacket, subdue the enemy and haul everyone's six out of hell.

"Nice place you got here." Brooklyn filed in last and dropped his gear beside the other duffels on the living room floor of EOD team member Billy Everrett's Kona, Hawaii, home. After getting everyone's butt out of the Afghan compound and safely returning to base with both hostages—the American journalist and the now bomb-free woman—

Brooklyn was more than glad the timing had worked out for him to join some of the guys on leave here on the Big Island. A last chance to be among his navy brothers that he didn't want to miss.

"The house is still a work in progress, but it's home." Billy pointed down the hall. "You've got four bedrooms to flip for. Mom always comes by to clean up the place for me when I'm back in Kona on leave. She texted that she changed the sheets for you guys, and I'm guessing there'll be a fridge full of food."

Nick, the EOD team leader, grabbed his bag to claim his room. Two steps behind him, Brent Callahan, a SEAL team mate, flashed his pearly whites. "And beer?"

"I said my mother." Billy rolled his eyes. "This isn't Australia. No locals leaving beer for sailors on this pier."

Kenny Yates, another of Brooklyn's SEAL team members, hefted his duffel and headed down the hallway. "How about women?"

Two steps behind him Brooklyn reached forward and slapped Kenny on the back. "Doubt his mom put those in the fridge either."

"Comedian." Kenny, originally from the Northeast, hip-checked Brooklyn as he walked by. In a blink, duffels were dropped, and the two men were on the ground.

"I swear, Brooklyn." Making his way across the room and down the hall in a heartbeat, Billy towered over the two tussling men. "One dent in my new walls and I'll have both your sixes on a platter."

"Sorry, man," Kenny mumbled, catching Brooklyn's

eye as he pushed to his feet. Having been on the same SEAL team for the last few years, words weren't required for communication. A turn, a lunge and a tackle later, all three were on the ground.

Brent emerged from the front bedroom and nearly got pulled into the fray. "I can think of better ways to work up a sweat, guys."

"He's right." Kenny eased back, and Billy took advantage of the shift in leverage to dump both SEALs on their sixes.

"Never mess with King Kona." Brushing his hands together, Billy spun about. "Clean up, and we'll hit the strip. It's no Gauntlet, but even you ugly frogs should be able to find a girl to take pity on you."

Showered, shaved and once again looking like a clean-cut sailor instead of a rebel insurgent, Brooklyn and his buddies walked into one of Billy's favorite local haunts. A splattering of pretty tourists decorated the place. Not near as many options as Honolulu and nothing at all like walking the famed foreign street known to sailors worldwide as The Gauntlet. But then again, few places were.

Brooklyn's introduction to The Gauntlet hadn't been long after earning his Trident and graduating from Coronado. The memory was still vivid. His team had gone in country on a reconnaissance mission and caught a ride offshore back to base on a Fast-Attack submarine. A fortuitous choice for transportation. En route, the sub had port call, and Brooklyn was introduced to The Gauntlet's hairpin strip of clubs and bars.

There, women of all shapes and sizes spilled onto the streets vying for their shot at an American sailor. Every few yards one of his group would be yanked aside and disappear into the open bars. A few would survive the barrage of women pawing and kissing to make it to the next one, usually sans a shirt, belt or some other article of clothing, and always bathed in lipstick and perfume.

Down to only a handful of men still walking, Brooklyn spotted a tall, lanky gal with long auburn hair. "I think I might be in the mood for a redhead."

One of the senior team members glanced over his shoulder and smiled. "Well, you'd better keep walking because that guy is probably a brunette."

"Hey." Brent waved his hand in front of Brooklyn's face snapping him back to the present. "Where did you go?"

Holding back a grin, he shrugged a shoulder. "Window-shopping."

All four friends cut him a curious glance before turning their attention back to a particularly interesting table of young ladies old enough to legally drink and young enough to make these sailor's night.

Across the room a few guys walked in the front door. One wore a Don't Tread on Me T-shirt, another sported an American flag tattoo and all had the regulation haircuts that screamed US Navy. Probably stationed at Pearl. And like Brooklyn and his buddies, creatures of habit. Give a sailor a day off, and he goes looking for beer and girls. Not a bad way to live.

"You're starting to worry me, Brooklyn." Billy pointed the neck of his beer bottle at him. "Wipe that crazy grin off your face."

"Aye, Chief." Brooklyn gave a weak salute. His last one. From now on he belonged to The Company. Six months ago he'd seen a mighty fine squadron of SEALs give up their lives due to bad intel. Intel provided by the CIA and their network of informants. So Brooklyn had requested separation from the US Navy and aligned himself with the very people who had gotten too many good men killed with planted information.

Next time Kenny, Brent and the rest of Brooklyn's former team members got intel through the CIA, Brooklyn would do his damnedest to make sure the info wouldn't get anyone killed. Or he'd die trying.

Two years later

The black-and-white from Miami PD pulled into Sharla Kramer's driveway.

Not again.

Tyler Hawk, former partner of her late husband, Danny, eased out of the driver seat. His expression blank, he opened the back door and out popped Sophia Garibaldi.

Not that Sharla had expected to see anyone else. At all of five foot two and a hundred pounds soaking wet, her grandmother still managed to cause more trouble than a rabbit in a lettuce patch. "Nana. Not again."

"Don't fuss. Tyler offered me a ride."

Sharla's gaze met Tyler's. Lips pressed tightly together, the six-foot-four policeman ran his hand across the back of his neck before speaking. "We picked her up at the mall."

"Nana," Sharla whined. "You promised."

"I didn't do anything." The older woman straightened her proud shoulders and lifted her stubborn chin. "That daft head of security called the police over a little misunderstanding."

Ever since Nana had retired to Florida to live with Sharla, "a little misunderstanding" had become the three most unsettling words in the English language.

"A shopper at the discount shoe store insisted your grandmother tried to pick her pocket. Said she saw Sophia's hand coming out of her purse just as the woman was about to pay for her purchases."

Sharla turned to her grandmother. "You had her wallet?"

"No," Tyler answered. "But the woman insisted she'd merely foiled your grandmother's attempt to steal it."

"Poppycock." Nana huffed. "If I'd wanted—"

"Yes, Nana, we know." Sharla cut off her grandmother before she could incriminate herself. Not that Tyler wasn't fully aware of the family history. He'd already been partnered with Danny when he had started dating Sharla and had witnessed firsthand the antics of her crazy family as they, one by one, retired—supposedly—to Florida. It was almost enough to make her want to move to Alaska. Or anyplace no one would be tempted to follow her.

Tyler waited until Sophia had crossed the doorway into the kitchen. "We've got lots of new rookies on board since… well, new guys who didn't know Danny."

Sharla bobbed her head. Tyler didn't have to say anything else. "I understand. Thanks for bringing her home. I'll go to the mall tomorrow after my shift at the hospital and have another talk with Mr. Delvecchio."

"You okay otherwise?"

Tyler flashed his trademark killer smile that would make most women weak in the knees. Especially if they were gazing into his crystal-blue eyes. A light, almost-gray shade of blue, they always twinkled with a little mischief no matter how serious the situation. But it had been Danny's reserved smile and warm chocolate eyes that had stolen her heart the first time he'd arrived at her apartment door with her great-aunts Alicia and Leticia in tow. "I'm fine. Thanks."

After Danny's funeral, Tyler had kept frequent tabs on her. At first she was glad for the company. Someone to talk to who knew Danny almost as well as she did. As the months passed by, she realized she couldn't keep living her life with Danny through shared memories. Eventually Tyler's calls and visits came less often. And now, three years later, she mostly only saw Tyler when he'd swoop in to rescue one of the great-aunts or, like tonight, her grandmother.

"You'll let me know if—"

"I need anything," Sharla finished for him with a smile. "Thanks again, Ty."

Front door latched shut, Sharla spun about and leaned back. What was she going to do with her nimble-fingered relatives? At least starting in a few days the next month would be surprise-free. While Great-Aunt Alicia visited her daughter in California for the summer, Nana and Great-Aunt Leticia were going on another Caribbean cruise and then planned to visit old friends in New York for a couple of weeks. As long as Nana and her former cohorts had an audience to entertain with their old stories, Sharla could rest assured they would stay out of trouble.

She hadn't heard the phone ring, but Nana's voice carried from the kitchen, "Oh my. Really?"

Upon closer observation, Sharla was not happy with the look on her grandmother's face.

"No, Ticia. Maybe I should—"

Sharla walked closer and leaned into her grandmother's side in an effort to eavesdrop on the phone conversation, but Nana wished her sister well and hung up. "What's the matter? Is there a problem with Nelda?"

"Not exactly. The baby decided to turn at the last minute. Doctors did a C-section. Ticia wants to stay and help while Nelda recovers."

The news wasn't as bad as Sharla had feared. Until it hit her why her grandmother's forehead was crinkled with concern. The cruise left on Thursday. No way Nelda would be a 100 percent by then for Leticia to go as planned.

In a snap Nana's expression cleared, a bright smile taking over her face. "Didn't your boss just say you had too many vacation days accumulated and you needed to take time off while he had the staff to cover for you?"

Actually, yes. She'd already penciled in two weeks while Nana was away. The perfect time to get in a little sun and tinker with some long-neglected household proj… "Oh, no."

"Of course. The cruise company said we could add passengers up to twenty-four hours before departure. You can have Leticia's place. Like the old days when your parents would be off on some adventure and the two of us would spend time on the Jersey shore."

"No, Nana." Absolutely not. No how. No way. Sharla was not spending two weeks trapped on a floating hotel in the middle of the ocean. "So not happening, Nana. There is nothing you can say to get me on that boat with you."

"Maybe Magda would like to join me."

Except that. The last thing Sharla needed was for her grandmother to reconnect with her old partner in crime. Heaven help her, it looked like she and Nana were going on a cruise.

Ignoring the burn still present in his side, Luke "Brooklyn" Chapman tried to relax into the stiff guest chair and propped his ankle across his thigh. The thick leather belt he'd worn that day when all hell had broken loose had slowed the knife enough to prevent any serious damage, especially since the stupid thing had been dipped in poison. Two years of deep undercover work had finally paid off. A little field needlework, some antidotal treatment and he was good to go.

Too bad the doc hadn't agreed.

"Thirty days. That's an order."

Disregarding the tug from the medic's stitches, Brooklyn shifted in place and flashed a cocky grin at his supervisor. "You can't give me an order. I'm not in the navy anymore."

"You won't be with anybody anymore if you don't take some downtime. I don't care how invincible you SEALs think you are. You are made of flesh and blood like everyone else. You cut. You bleed. You die. I don't want to see your face or hear your name for thirty days."

In the navy, as SEALs on standby, Brooklyn and his men were limited to two beers a day and an hour-long leash, never allowed to be more than sixty minutes away from base. A few days of true R & R when they would be free to indulge in all the booze and women they could handle was always embraced with much anticipation. But usually after only a few days of rest and recreation, he'd been ready to go back to work. And not just busy work or physical training. Something worthy of his time and all that constant PT. "I'll take a couple of days."

"Thirty."

"But—"

"Listen, Brooklyn." Phil Conway leaned forward on his desk. "I know you want to see all these bastards fry as much as any of us."

More. Under the umbrella of the CIA, in a joint task

force with the navy commanded by Admiral Cartwright, Brooklyn, along with a former ranger and another spook, had infiltrated the terrorist cell believed to have been behind the faulty intel that had gotten a squadron of SEALs killed almost three years ago.

The recent firefight that had left Brooklyn with a knife in his gut had also taken out the SOBs responsible for the death of his fellow SEALs. But there was always another terrorist waiting to step up and annihilate "the American infidels." When the terrorists took R & R, then so would he.

"You are running on caffeine and adrenaline," Conway continued. "Something's got to give sooner or later, and it's not going to be on my watch."

For a spook Conway was a decent guy, but he didn't get it. Brooklyn could remind his boss from now till the next millennium what every SEAL endured for months of basic training. Constant harassing by professional warriors with one objective: eliminate the weak. Only the strongest and smartest survived Hell Week and BUD/S. Long torturous runs in the soft sand. Midnight swims in the cold Pacific. Arduous obstacle courses. Never-ending calisthenics. Days without sleep. Always being cold, wet and miserable.

And the training didn't stop there. The training never stopped. In the real world, lack of sleep and physical endurance was a way of life. SEALs thrived on stress and chaos. He didn't need thirty days with nothing to do.

"Got anyplace you've always wanted to go?" Conway asked. "Family you haven't seen for a while?"

Some downtime home in New York with the family would be good. Even with his mother hovering over him, it would be great to see his sisters and nieces and nephews. And it had been a while since he'd had a decent lasagna. But thirty days?

He could always throw a dart at a map and see where it landed. There were plenty of possible destinations where people weren't trying to kill each other. King Kona's family owned a dive shop on the Big Island. Going there for a few days could be a nice break. Billy always bragged about the weather, the diving, and how great his family was. Of course his sisters would be off-limits. A guy didn't hook up with a buddy's sister; that was an unbreakable code. But Brooklyn couldn't wrap his mind around the idea of lying under a palm tree and watching the coconuts fall.

Conway sat back and steepled his fingers under his chin. "My wife and I are booked on a cruise, but her mother has decided now would be a good time to have the knee replacement surgery she's been putting off for two years. Martha won't leave her mother. We're supposed to sail Thursday afternoon. Thirteen nights. Too late for a refund. You'd have the cabin to yourself."

"I can't—"

"You'd be doing me a favor. If you take my place, I can pass the bill on to accounting. Otherwise I have to eat the cost."

Thirteen days of poolside lounging. The Hawaiian coconuts were looking more appealing. Except... ship pools had babes in bikinis. After two years in another world, he wouldn't object to skipping Rest and going directly for Recreation. "Okay. I'll do it. But you'll owe me."

Conway's lips tipped up in a much-too-satisfied grin.

Somewhere deep down in his gut Luke was sure he'd just been had.

MEET CHRIS

Author of dozens of contemporary novels, including the award winning Aloha Series, Chris Keniston lives in suburban Dallas with her husband, two human children, and two canine children. Though she loves her puppies equally, she admits being especially attached to her German Shepherd rescue. After all, even dogs deserve a happily ever after.

More on Chris and her books can be found at www.chriskeniston.com.

Follow Chris on facebook at ChrisKenistonAuthor or on twitter @ckenistonauthor.

Join Chris' newsletter! Enjoy inside peeks and photographs from Chris' world and stories. Some times she'll thank her subscribers with a free copy of a new 99 cent flirt.

Please, if you enjoyed reading Love Walks In, consider helping other readers find the Aloha Romance series by taking a moment to leave a review. Reviews are a blessing to authors and readers alike. Even just a few words will do! Thank you.

www.ingramcontent.com/pod-product-compliance
Lightning Source LLC
Chambersburg PA
CBHW030841200726
48285CB00007B/2512